THE CHRISTMAS TREE FARM

A HOPE HERRING COZY MYSTERY
BOOK 12

J. A. WHITING

NELL MCCARTHY

Copyright 2023 J.A. Whiting and Whitemark Publishing

Cover copyright 2023 Signifer Book Design

Formatting by Signifer Book Design

Proofreading by Donna Rich: donnarich@me.com

This book is a work of fiction. Names, characters, places, or incidents are products of the author's imagination or are used fictitiously. Any resemblance to locales, actual events, or persons, living or dead, is entirely coincidental.

All rights reserved.

No part of this publication can be reproduced or transmitted in any form or by any means, electronic or mechanical, without permission in writing from J. A. Whiting.

To hear about new books and book sales, please sign up for my mailing list at:
jawhiting.com

❃ Created with Vellum

With thanks to our readers

Dream big

1

"Did you know that North Carolina has thirteen hundred Christmas tree farms that produce fifty million trees?"

Hope frowned. "This is September. Christmas is still three months away."

The drive home from the schools where Hope taught and Cori attended was short. The September afternoon was still warm and the car's air conditioner hummed along. The trees had not yet started to turn. It would be another month before colors arrived. That was the difference between Castle Park, North Carolina and Columbus, Ohio, where Hope and her daughter had come from. Winters were shorter and warmer here and autumn arrived later. All in all, Hope preferred the milder winters.

"I know," Cori said. "It's just a factoid like the one that says almost all the Christmas trees raised here are Fraser firs. We ship them around the world."

"Good to know. Is this part of some idea you have about Christmas murders?"

"No, no, after last year, I think we should stay home for Christmas."

"I thought you were afraid of the curse if we stayed home."

"I am, but the curse isn't dependent on location. We proved that last year with the murder in Ohio. So, if there's going to be a murder around Christmas, we should solve it from the comfort of our own home."

"We? I wasn't aware that you solved last year's murder," Hope told her daughter.

Cori glanced at her mother. "Mom, I am a valuable partner in your crime investigations and solutions. After all, we were nearly blown up together."

"That's true." Hope turned the SUV onto a side road. "Is all of this leading up to something? Is there something you want?"

"I'm not aiming for anything more than what I have."

"I agree that staying home this year for the holidays is a good choice, but are you expecting an invitation from Lottie and her parents to travel somewhere?"

"Not this year, but I think Lottie's mom will probably want to send you to Fiji or something. After all, you kept her out of jail." Recently, Lottie's mom had been a suspect in a crime, and Hope helped prove her innocence.

"She didn't commit a crime, so she didn't deserve to go to jail."

"You still saved her," Cori pointed out. "Did you know there's a Christmas tree farm not far from here?"

"You can't get a Christmas tree in September."

"No, but you can pick one out now." Cori fiddled with her long brown braid.

"Oh, really?"

"I read online that you can choose one, and they'll put your name on it, and cut it and bundle it the day before you want to pick it up. What could be better than that?"

Hope glanced at her daughter. "You want to shop for a Christmas tree already?"

"Why not? Think of all the hassle you'll miss. It's warm now, so you won't be cold. The tree will be waiting for us. We'll miss the Christmas rush and any price hikes. It's the next best thing to chopping down your own tree."

"Let me guess. You and Lottie will both go and help with the choosing."

"We can't very well leave it in our parents' hands."

Hope laughed. "How do you know all this? I smell an alternative reason."

"River Soames. He's a year older than me, and his dad owns the Christmas tree farm."

"I see, and this River Soames must be good looking, right?"

"I'm allowed to look at boys, Mom." Cori watched the scenery go by through the car window.

"Yes, you've reached that age when all the magic in life disappears. It's time to be serious," Hope kidded.

Cori rolled her eyes. "I'm not that bad."

"Not yet, not yet. Please try to remember that I was your age once. I haven't forgotten everything."

"Those were the dark ages, Mom. Things are different now."

"I agree, but human nature is not. I believe you're probably doomed to make the same mistakes most of us made at your age."

"A teachable moment?" the teen asked.

"I believe you are trying to teach *me*. You've successfully hidden your true motive behind a veil of Christmas trees."

Cori laughed. "One of the best ploys in chess is to get your opponent fixated on your queen. If you can place it just so, you can then mount an attack from another direction."

"I'll remember that."

"So, we'll go Christmas tree hunting?"

"I don't see why not."

"Can Luke come?" Cori asked. Hope had been seeing Luke Donlan casually, as neither of them wanted to rush things. They'd meet for dinner, a bike ride, get coffee, or take a walk or a hike together. Hope and Luke enjoyed one another's company, and she could see it moving forward someday. But that someday was way off in the future.

"Luke is away working on a project. He won't be back for about a week." Luke owned a landscaping business, and due to his reputation for fine work, he was in demand across the state.

"Bummer," Cori said. "It's always fun when he comes with us. Can Lottie come along?"

"Are you two planning to gang up on poor River?"

"She's my wing-girl."

Hope laughed. "That's cute, but I agree there's safety in numbers."

"When can we go?"

"Soon. I'm guessing River has become a desirable object at school."

"I never said that."

"I'm your mother. I keep tabs."

"A girl has to dream, right?"

"Dreaming is fine—as long as it doesn't interfere with real work or life."

"Roger that."

Hope pulled into their driveway, and she and her daughter got out and went inside through the back door where they greeted Bijou, their big fluffy brown and white cat. The century-old house met Hope with the usual creaks and squeaks, but it was as good a house as she had ever owned. All amenities were included, even her office in the attic, and that office came equipped with a unique feature ... Max.

Maximillian Johnson was the house's resident ghost. He had been haunting the place ever since his murder a hundred years in the past. He vowed not to leave until he had determined who killed him. Since the attack had come from behind, Max didn't know who had done it, until he and Hope were able to solve the mystery through research and smarts. He latched onto the house because to leave it would be to move on, and he was not ready to do that.

Hope found the ghost in a familiar spot, right in front of her office computer.

"How's it going?" She placed her briefcase on the floor next to the desk.

"I have met an historian online who is helping with my research."

"I noticed your deerslayer hat and pipe. Sherlock Holmes, I presume?"

"Correct, Mrs. Herring. I have renewed my single-minded search for the truth. I don't know how long my resolve will last. The Internet is a siren that beckons me at every turn."

Max wore his black, burial suit with its white shirt and black tie. He hadn't aged since his death, which seemed pretty standard for a ghost. He had come with the house which proved invaluable to Hope. He was the best security system in the world.

"I wish you success, Max. All is well here?"

"We are at that end of summer, the autumn cusp. It is a pleasant time of the year, although it will get better after a frost kills off the mosquitos and lowers the humidity."

"When you were alive, when did you count autumn being officially here?"

"I always marked the week when the cormorants arrived."

"Cormorants?"

"Ducks, I believe. They would arrive at Lake Lamont when the temperatures dropped. I never knew where they came from, some place up north, I assume. They wintered here for the most part, fishing in the lake and perching in the trees. It seemed to me they spent more time in the trees than they did in the water. When they returned north, I knew winter was over."

"I'll remember that."

"Do you need the computer, Mrs. Herring?"

"Not yet, Max. After dinner, I'll need it. I have some email to answer and grades to input."

"Just let me know when you're ready."

Hope returned to the kitchen, but it was too early to start dinner, so she poured herself a glass of Merlot and went outside to the patio. There were woods at the back of the property, which provided Hope with some privacy. Occasionally, a deer or two emerged from the woods and tracked across her yard, heading for the denser trees on the outskirts of Castle Park. The county teemed with deer. Unfortunately, there wasn't a week that passed without a vehicle-deer accident. They were dangerous on the roads, but a pleasure to watch in the yard.

The green and tan striped umbrella provided some shade, which was always a good thing to find in Castle Park. She glanced up and saw a hawk circling above the woods. When Hope first moved south, she marveled at the number of birds, big birds. She knew the lakes and ponds didn't cater to only cormorants and geese; herons, buzzards, egrets, and bald eagles were around also. There were territorial skirmishes between birds, since the best fishing spots were always in demand. Birds had to eat all the time. Luckily, the lakes and ponds almost never froze over.

Hope's thoughts turned from the birds, ducks, and deer to Cori. Her daughter had begun to notice boys. That meant she'd entered a new phase of growing up. Hope knew it was a natural phase. Every male and female went through it sooner or later. Yet, the addition of the "boy variable" complicated Cori's and Hope's lives. New rules would have to be agreed on and put in place. A bit more oversight would be needed. A lapse of judgment could change Cori's life forever. No mother wanted her daughter or son to choose poorly. It was better to put off some things.

Could Hope convince Cori of that?

Hope was not so old that she'd forgotten her own rite of passage. High school could be a mine field filled with missteps that destroyed reputations and future careers. Some of her classmates shifted their focus from classes to popularity. It was a must to wear the latest fashion, embrace the latest fad. Everyone seemed to be working on their outsides, and ignoring their insides.

Hope had not been the exception. She simply didn't join the girls in the outer orbits. Her father continually asked her if the things she bought or acquired actually made her life better. Most of the time, she admitted she was just trying to fit in, gain friends. He reminded her that friends didn't come with new shoes or hair dye. If they did, everyone would be popular. Hope later wished she had listened more closely. At the time, she often considered her parents to be pests.

Cori.

Hope's trip through young adulthood was over, but Cori's was just beginning. She needed to focus on her daughter. She would have to walk a fine line between smothering and monitoring. In fact, she knew she would never be able to hold the line. She would swing back and forth, making a mistake one way and then the other. The moments when she was exactly balanced would be few. That was how life worked. A pendulum was exactly vertical for only an instant.

Part of Hope wanted to lock Cori away until she turned twenty-five and possessed more common sense, but that was impossible.

Another part of Hope wanted to release Cori and step back. Allow the girl to find her own way, make her own mistakes. That was tempting, but it constituted being an irresponsible parent. Pitfalls and bogs appeared in every direction. Hope supposed she would muddle through, as she always did. She couldn't control the future. She couldn't even control the present.

When Hope was in high school, she would prepare for special conversations. Mostly they were chats with boys. She rehearsed the dialogue in her head. She would say this, and he would answer that, and then, she would say something incredibly witty and charming. Only, the conversations never happened that way. The boys never knew their lines. They never set the stage for her clever responses. Hope wasted precious time prepping for chats that never happened. Worse, she didn't learn that she couldn't control both sides of the conversation until she was in college. Would she discover how to deal with Cori, only after Cori moved out of the house?

Probably.

Hope sighed. The hawk had disappeared. There were no deer emerging from the trees and loping across her lawn. The sky was still blue, but the sun was setting on the other side of the house. She guessed Max was busy surfing the net, chasing down every bit of click bait offered to him. She needed to start dinner, but she hesitated. The light was too perfect, the temperature just right, and the mosquitos hadn't yet arrived for their evening meal. She could afford to sit a few more minutes and contemplate her muddling.

The first blip on Cori's radar was River Soames. Hope wanted to find out more about him and his family and their Christmas tree farm. She had a date to choose a Christmas tree for later pickup, but the tree was really just a ruse. Cori was the object of the adventure—Cori, Lottie, and ... River.

2

Saturday morning found Hope making cakes in the back kitchen of the Butter Up Bakery. When she first moved to Castle Park, Edsel Morgan, the owner of the bakery, needed a cake baker. Hope took the job, and as a bonus, she and Edsel had become friends. The two women liked each other. When Hope solved the murder of Edsel's niece, their friendship had strengthened. Edsel acknowledged that bringing the killer to justice brought her peace of mind.

Hope added the finishing touches to the wedding cake destined for Krissy and Roy, whoever they were. She knew the newlyweds would think the cake was delicious. Butter Up, and Hope had established a certain reputation for the best cakes in southeastern North Carolina.

What Hope remembered best about the cakes was the very first one she made. People thought she had poisoned it on purpose. She'd been forced to find the killer, or face prison. She had come a long way since then.

Sitting at a desk in the corner of the backroom, Cori looked up from the chess game she was playing on her laptop computer. "Can Lottie come over when we get home?"

"I don't see why not. Do you want her to stay for dinner?"

"I don't know, maybe. I think she needs to get out of the house. Her parents are starting to crack down."

"Why?"

"She's having problems with math, and they're all over her. They think she's going to be a rocket scientist or something. She's not. I know that, and she knows that, but her parents don't want to accept it."

"Is Lottie trying at math?"

"She says she is."

"What do you think?" Hope swirled some frosting over the sides of the cake.

"I don't know. She doesn't do her homework. She used to copy mine, but I stopped letting her. She wasn't happy about that, but she can't learn if she doesn't do it herself."

"You did exactly what a good friend should do."

"I hope so. You know how much I'd like to help her."

"Cori, show her how to do the math, walk her through the steps. Feeding her answers doesn't help. I hope you believe that."

"Yeah, but it's still not easy."

"Being responsible is rarely easy. Does this problem have anything to do with River?"

Cori shrugged.

"Come on, Cori, I know there are more than a couple of girls infatuated with River. Is Lottie one of them?"

"Yeah, she is. River smiled at her yesterday, and Lottie was gaga for the rest of the day."

"Is he playing her?"

"I think so. But then, he smiles at me, too. What about that?"

"I think he might be flirting with a lot of girls, or he's just very friendly. Is he smart?"

Cori frowned. "Not book smart. I think there are

a couple of girls in his class that feed him homework, but he's not stupid. He knows stuff."

"He's clever?"

"Yeah, that's what he is. I don't know if I trust him though."

"That's up to you. Use your judgment."

"He's too good looking for that."

Hope laughed. "I think there are studies that say attractive people are assumed to be smarter and better leaders than the not-so-handsome people."

Cori frowned. "That's very wrong."

"Nope, that's life. The prettiest male cardinal gets the attention of all the female cardinals."

"Yeah, it happens like that."

When they left the bakery and reached home, Hope headed up to the attic office. Max, dressed in a jogging outfit, was at the computer, and Bijou was sleeping on the desk next to him.

"Any luck with your Internet searches?" Hope asked.

Max shook his head. "Not unless you mean the comfort of this jogging suit. It's really nice. I am genuinely amazed by modern fabrics. In my day, we had cotton, cotton, wool, and more cotton. You would not believe how much time was spent just ironing clothes."

"Modern conveniences are amazing. When you think about fridges, stoves, microwaves, dishwashers, the average workday for a husband and wife was probably cut in half."

"As you are no doubt aware, Mrs. Herring, children in my era had to work as hard as their parents. No one was above hard toil. I remember my own youth on the family farm. Dawn woke me, and darkness meant sleep. In between, I milked and baled hay and planted and harvested. On rainy days, we repaired what had broken under the strain. There were never enough hours or food. I think that's what amazes me about today, the abundance of food. If you had told me what the horn of plenty would produce today, I would have called you a liar. It is truly a miracle."

"We take our food supply for granted. I read once where the supermarkets have basically three days of food available. If they aren't resupplied in three days, the shelves are empty."

"No root cellars or cured meats?"

"I'm afraid not. Oh, people have pantries filled with canned goods and some staples, but few are prepared for an extended disruption of the supply chain."

"That is a dangerous position to be in, Mrs. Herring."

"It is, but unless there is some sort of natural disaster, flood, hurricane, blizzard, the system is very reliable."

"I suppose your neighbors would offer to share under adverse circumstances."

"They would. But, let's not be Pollyannas. If things became really rough, we would revert to jungle rules. You know the mentality ... feed your own and worry about the others later."

"I am very familiar with that attitude. On the high seas, it was often every man for himself, even if cooperation would prove more useful."

"I'd rather not think about that, Max. I'll hang onto my belief in the continuation of what we have. Maybe, we'll make it even better."

"I shall share your optimism."

"Cori has Lottie coming over this evening so I'll stay downstairs for now. Enjoy your time at the computer."

"I have discovered that I have an almost insatiable thirst for information. Odd, that I hadn't been so curious while I was alive."

"Circumstances change," Hope told him with a smile. "I'll see you a little later."

After returning to the first floor of the house, Hope stopped by her daughter's bedroom where she found Cori and Lottie on the bed, phones in hand, busy tapping out messages.

"I hope you two are sending messages to other people and not to each other," Hope kidded.

"Duh," Cori said. "If we text each other, it's to share a pic or a vid."

"If we want to talk, we talk," Lottie said.

Lottie's head was shaved on one side and featured coal black hair on the other. Lottie's hair was not naturally so dark, and the contrast with her white scalp was dramatic. Hope was reminded of a Disney character whose jet-black hair was interrupted by a pure white streak. Perhaps, Lottie had copied the look.

"That's good," Hope said. "I once read a science fiction story where the characters no longer spoke. They communicated on devices like our phones, and they lost their voices entirely. Of course, sarcasm is limited when you remove facial expressions and voice inflections. Obviously, misunderstandings led to battles and, well, disaster."

"Can't happen with us, Mom," Cori said. "We're not that stupid."

"I hope not. There may come a time when your

phones will no longer work, and you'll be forced to talk to each other."

"The grid and Internet are not going to disappear, Mrs. Herring," Lottie said. "They're forever."

"Nothing is forever, Lottie. I'm sure when the telegraph was introduced, people thought it would last forever. Telegrams are a thing of the past, as are transistor radios, Model T Fords, and gaslights. One day, you might have an entire phone implanted in your brains. You won't even need a device in order to communicate and surf."

"That would be kind of cool," Lottie said.

"I'm not so sure," Cori interjected. "You get something in your brain like that, and people will figure out a way to control it. Then, you don't know what might be implanted in there."

"I still think it would be cool. Hey, Mrs. Herring, who's the man in your office?"

Hope stared as her heart rate increased. "Man in my office?"

"I heard you talking to him. I didn't mean to eavesdrop."

"Oh, that was someone on my computer. We were doing a zoom meeting." Hope didn't for a minute believe Lottie wasn't eavesdropping. Why else would she be anywhere close to the attic?

"Oh, yeah, I didn't think of that. He sounded pretty cool."

"Just another teacher. Hey, what do you two want for dinner?"

"Pizza," Lottie said.

"Pizza," Cori echoed.

"Good enough. Pizza Corner, or do you want carryout?"

"The Corner," Cori said.

"How about the Pizza Inn," Lottie suggested. "I heard it was good."

"Pizza Inn?" Cori asked. "Why there?"

"You know." Lottie gave her friend a knowing look.

"Oh, right," Cori answered. "I'm with Lottie, Mom. Pizza Inn is fine with me."

Hope could only guess at the attraction of the Pizza Inn. It was probably a boy, probably River. That made sense. The girls would eat there on the off chance that the boy would appear. He might not yet be old enough to work there. She thought about asking the girls, but they would probably deny everything. That was a good strategy, just in case he didn't show up. They could always say they just picked a different pizza place for a change.

"All right, the Pizza Inn it is. We'll leave in an

hour."

Hope retreated to her office, where Max still sat at the computer.

"I think we need to be more careful," Hope said. "Lottie overheard us talking."

"I might have known, Mrs. Herring. However, she had no business coming up here."

"I agree. Just to be safe, when she's in the house, let's keep our conversations short and quiet."

"Indeed. I shall be the epitome of silence. I will also keep tabs on the girl before she becomes a liability."

"Indeed."

The Pizza Inn was decidedly newer. It had more lighting, more tile, more noise, and lacked the shadowy corners Hope preferred. It did feature a children's room filled with tiny slides, a bouncy net filled with multi-colored plastic balls, and a maze of sorts.

The menu was retrieved by phone by taking a pic of a pattern on the table. Cori and Lottie pulled up the menu in seconds. Hope merely waited until they had chosen something, before she looked at Cori's phone. While she scanned choices and prices, the girls jumped up and ran to another table where their friends were busy on their phones.

Hope was familiar with the move. She supposed she should start looking around for dinner partners. The girls would soon prefer their own friends. And when Cori started driving... Hope didn't finish the thought.

The menu had included red wine, which Hope now sipped. The wine wasn't all that good, but it was passable. She noted that beer was served also, but no mixed drinks. That was probably a good thing as the restaurant catered to families. There was no bar. She picked up her phone and immediately put it down. She was not going to imitate the teenagers, who seemed attached to their mobile devices. Hope wondered if they ever put down the phone, except to charge it. If her parents had been there, Hope guessed they would have frowned at the phone use. Probably more than any other invention, cell phones signaled a retreat from talk. In a way, it was kind of sad.

She visually checked on Lottie and Cori, who were still engaged with their friends. Hope was going to give them one more minute before she called them back and made them order. She wasn't about to spend several hours eating pizza and drinking wine. Besides, the Saturday night crowd filled the place. The waitstaff, no doubt, appreciated people who ate and left.

The new family that entered seemed to dampen the noise for a few seconds. They were ordinary enough. The father in a plaid shirt, worn jeans, and work boots; a plump mother in shorts, festive top, and sandals; and a son in jeans and black tee, handsome for his age with dark, unruly hair. Hope guessed he was about sixteen and was athletic from his build. As the family passed Cori and Lottie, the two girls stared. Hope guessed that the boy was the reason the girls wanted to come to the Pizza Inn.

The family settled at a table across the room. They'd hardly sat before Cori and Lottie rushed back to Hope's table. They both sat in chairs where they could watch the new family.

"Do you know them?" Hope asked.

"Who?" Cori answered.

"I think it's pretty obvious, but I'll play along. The family that just walked in, the one with the teenager in a black shirt."

"I didn't notice," Lottie said.

"I'm not so old or so inattentive to not recognize the heart throb better known as River."

Cori looked at Lottie, who looked back at her.

Hope laughed.

3

Hope decided to forego any discussion with Cori concerning River Soames. She could see why the schoolgirls talked about him ... he was handsome, and he would probably get more handsome as he aged. He had one of those faces. River would have his choice of the girls in high school and maybe even in college. Was he smart? Hope didn't know, and she was certain Cori didn't care. Intelligence was one of those things often overlooked when boy meets girl. For some reason, teens always thought that other teens wouldn't change. It was like dreaming about someone from the past. Dream characters never changed. Not until they were seen a second time.

After school the next day, Cori retreated to her room. There was a big science quiz the next day, and she wanted to ace it. Acing the quiz would automatically give her a pass on the next quiz. Hope questioned the logic, but it wasn't her class. She left Cori to her studies and climbed the steps to the attic with Bijou trotting behind. She found Max, in his jogging suit, staring out the window.

"Internet not working?" Hope asked.

He turned, and she recognized his troubled face. "I believe I must ask a favor, Mrs. Herring."

"Certainly, Max. What is it?"

"I was surfing today, and I came across the library at the University of North Carolina, Chapel Hill. A very fine institution, if one can believe the accolades laid upon it."

"One of the best schools in the nation and certainly the crown jewel of the North Carolina system."

"Exactly. Well, their library contains an unfathomable number of books and manuscripts and newspapers and whatnot. No single person could ever read everything. Not in a thousand years."

Hope nodded. "I would venture that every major university in the country has a similar library. Of course, between universities, there would be a good deal of duplication, but every university possesses some unique titles and authors."

"As one would guess. The North Carolina library contains a diary section. I have overlooked it in the past. They have segregated the diaries by state, and, of course, the North Carolina section is by far the largest. They have a magnificent list of diaries from the Civil War. People were much more given to writing diaries than they are today. I must assume most people keep an online diary, if they keep one at all."

"You're right, Max. People don't call them diaries anymore. They're called journals. Most English teachers try to prod their students into keeping journals, but they don't often succeed. Students believe they have brilliant ideas. They just don't always put them down on paper."

"Yes, well, I was browsing through the list of diaries, and I came across a name I recognized ... Haley June Watson. If you think back, you will remember that she was on my original list of suspects."

"Oh, yes, I do recognize the name, Max."

"If you recall, her husband, my partner, died, and I settled with her according to the partnership agreement. In my mind, I was generous. In hers, I cheated her out of a great sum of money. I won't go into details. Suffice it to say, I wish to read her diary, as it might contain a clue to my murder. However, I cannot make the trip. I know you're wondering if the diary has been put online. The answer is no, not yet. So, I'm asking if you might make a trip for me."

"Of course, I will, Max. But we solved your murder. Why are you interested in what she wrote in her diary?"

Max's face was serious. "What if we are wrong about who killed me?"

"I don't think we got it wrong, but I'll drive over, read the diary, and take notes. How is that?"

"I don't believe you have to read the entire diary, as I doubt she had any kind words for me. If you'll read the entries slightly before and slightly after my death, that should prove sufficient."

"Diaries are generally not overly long. Only famous people like Winston Churchill and the like wrote extensively during their lives. Most of us simply never take the time."

"I appreciate this very much, and there is no need to hurry. I have waited this long. I can wait longer."

"This weekend, Max. I'll show Cori the campus, and I'll take a gander at that diary."

Hope broached the topic over dinner. "I want to

make a trip to Chapel Hill. There's some original research I need to do."

"Cool. What about? Are you writing a book or something?"

"Not a book. Max thinks we might have the wrong killer. He worries that someone else may have killed him. Someone's diary is located in the university library and he'd like me to read it over to be sure we named the real criminal."

"Diaries are like stories, aren't they?"

Hope nodded. "They can be the story of someone's life, yes."

"There's a girl at school named Cassandra Rimes. She tells the same boring stories over and over. I try to listen, but it's really hard. I want to finish her sentences for her."

"Don't do that. Just smile and listen. Consider it a lesson in good manners."

"You and your lessons. Will they ever end?"

"Certainly, as soon as you stop being my daughter." Hope smiled.

Cori laughed. "Don't tempt me."

"Be careful what you wish for. The ancient Greeks believed that the gods punished humans by giving them what they asked for, but there was always a catch."

"That I find hard to believe."

"Then, you don't know the story of King Midas and the Midas touch."

"Do I have to listen?"

"You asked for it. Besides, it's a short fable."

"If you insist."

"I do. Midas was a king, and he wanted a gift from the gods. Being greedy, he asked that he be granted the power to turn anything he touched into gold."

"Anything at all?"

"Anything."

"Cool." Cori liked what she was hearing.

"So, it would seem. What Midas and most people wouldn't realize is that anything and everything he touched turned into gold. He hugged his wife, and she turned into gold."

"Oops."

"He touched his daughter, and she turned into gold."

Cori half-smiled. "She was probably a pain anyway."

Hope went on, "When he tried to eat, the bite of an apple turned to gold in his mouth."

"Uh oh. That's a problem."

"He couldn't eat, he couldn't drink, but he was

surrounded by gold. He had gained a fortune beyond all imagination, and he had lost what was truly valuable ... life."

"He should have put in some kind of escape clause. I mean, he needed a better attorney."

"So the lesson is, be careful what you wish for. All right, I have a very light schedule on Saturday at the bakery. I'll be home by 10am, and we can take off for Chapel Hill. It's roughly two hours, a little longer if we throw in lunch."

"Can Lottie come? I mean, if you're going to be busy in the library, I'll just have to twiddle my thumbs or something."

"Do you even know how to twiddle your thumbs?"

"That's beside the point. If Lottie comes, I'll have someone to explore with."

"All right, she can come, if her mother says it's okay. But, you both have to agree to abide by a few rules."

"Ah, the Midas touch thing."

"You can be left behind with a babysitter if you'd rather stay at home."

Cori sat straighter. "I'm listening."

"It's a public university, so the campus is open. That does not mean it's safe. First rule is that the two of you stay together ... always. No one goes off on her own. Think of yourselves as conjoined twins."

"Yuck. Is there such a thing?"

"Look it up. Stay out of the dorms, sororities, and fraternities. They're not for you, and you have no experience with them. Bookstores are fine, and I'm guessing the two of you can find a place to grab a bite if you get hungry. The library will be open, but I doubt you'll go there. Of course, you can walk all over campus and look around. I know it's a little early to scope out campuses, but take the opportunity to learn more about the school. Who knows, you might want to spend your college years there. Do not, do not leave campus. I believe there are some bars and such right off the campus. Avoid them. Last, you have to check in with me every hour. A text will do. You do not have to tell me where you are, but it will make me feel a little better if you do."

"Do we get ankle monitors, too?" Cori kidded.

"Don't tempt me."

Cori drew a finger across her lips. Hope knew the signal. The subject had been finalized.

Adele, Lottie's mother, was only too glad to turn Lottie over to Hope for a day. Adele and Lottie had reached the abrasive level of their relationship.

While Lottie was still obedient, to a degree, she argued about every little thing.

"I always thought Cori was the more advanced of the girls," Adele said. "But it seems Lottie has beaten your daughter to the terrible teen years."

"I'm sure Cori is within hailing distance," Hope said. "I'll make sure they stay safe."

"If you lose her, just come on home. It will be less trouble without her," Adele kidded.

Saturday dawned clear and warm, and when Hope returned from the bakery, she said goodbye to Max, loaded Cori and Lottie into the SUV, and set off for Chapel Hill. She listened as the girls chattered for a little while, then, they went silent as they reverted to their phones.

That left Hope to ponder what she might find when she reached the library. More than likely, the diaries would hold nothing of significance. It would be just one more rabbit hole she and Max had explored. In a way, she felt sorry for her ghost. He was over a century removed from his murder, and he still wasn't sure who had killed him. Hope was pretty certain they had solved the mystery, but she understood his concern that they had gotten it wrong.

She managed to find a parking space not too far from the library, and she and the girls had their last review of the rules. If they got into trouble, they were to call. If there was danger involved, 911 would be dialed. They were to take no chances they could avoid. They knew all the rules about not going off with some man to search for his lost puppy or even to help someone who appeared injured. If that someone was injured, then call 911. Simple and efficient. The girls promised to stay in touch and keep out of trouble. That was easy for them to say, but Hope knew better. Trouble sometimes blocked a path.

The special section librarian smiled when Hope introduced herself. Hope guessed the librarian didn't have a lot of customers. It turned out that there were actually six diaries from the life of Haley June Watson. They were frail, as the paper in that era was not designed to last for centuries. Hope was given white cotton gloves and instructed how to gently handle the pages. Speed was the enemy. Slow was smooth, and smooth was fast enough. She was escorted to a small, climate-controlled room. Preservation was the goal. Hope assured the librarian she wouldn't be there long, and that brought a smile to the woman's face.

"Everyone says that," the librarian said. "Before they start reading. Enjoy."

Hope laid out the diaries and stared for a few moments. The books spanned the year of Max's death. She wondered if she needed to start with the oldest diary or the one from the year of his murder. The simplest strategy was to start with the death year, but that didn't seem like the best way. Perhaps, Hope needed to gain an insight into the woman's mind and style. She doubted that Haley June would write a confession in a diary that could be used in a court of law. The woman would probably disguise a confession as something else so that she could always claim an alternate interpretation. Hope chose the year before Max's year of death.

As instructed, Hope carefully opened the diary to the middle. A random date would do. She stared. The penmanship was poor and scratchy. Why did she think entries would be typed or printed? She told herself she was spoiled.

The first entry was: "I went to Henderson's Market today. I despise Henderson, but his is the only market worth anything."

4

Hope worked her way through the first diary, and it was hard work. She had problems with the penmanship, the structure, and the vocabulary. Haley June wrote in English, but it wasn't the English of the 21st century. Yet, by the time Hope reached the end of the diary, she felt she had grasped the essence of the woman's style.

What the writing revealed was a person who despised most of the people around her, even if she forced a smile whenever she ran into them. The disdain was written into the descriptions. Haley June didn't like many people, and she especially hated ... Max.

Hope opened the next diary which was written two months before Max's murder. If there was a plan afoot, Haley might well confide it to her diary. Hope didn't think the woman was so stupid as to describe the crime in detail, but she might leave a hint or two. People often thought they could cleverly disguise a reference so that no one would ever guess.

Those people were often wrong.

Hope did not hurry. Skimming at this point was the wrong tactic. She needed to wade through the entries. She needed to decipher the initials that were used—if she could decipher them. She realized that Haley June used initials only for relatives or people she knew well. She would use full names for many other people. Hope supposed it was a way to keep things straight.

Many of the entries were mundane, simply the ebb and flow of daily life. Occasionally, Haley June would go off on a tangent, writing about how she hated some people, particularly Max, who had deprived her of her money. She seemed to blame all her ills on being cheated out of what she believed was rightfully hers. Hope looked for something that would be a clue to a conspiracy. She didn't believe Haley June had the wherewithal to kill Max on her own. But, Haley June might well hire someone to get it done. Or, maybe she could persuade someone to do the job.

The entry two days before the murder seemed to tell something.

"Sometimes, I feel like a schoolgirl again. I'm home, and there is to be a cotillion on Saturday, and I would love to attend. I know I cannot, as I am a widow and not allowed to have fun. Even if I dared, I have no dress that would fit my need. That could be rectified, had I what I deserve. Maximillian, the devil, swindled me out of more than just money. He took part of my soul. I live for the day he pays for his crimes. I pray that day is not far away. Perhaps, the future will answer my prayers sooner rather than later."

Was there something Haley June knew that she wasn't putting down on paper? Max wasn't ill. There was no reason to expect him to keel over at a moment's notice. Did she mean that she expected to outlive Max? Hope turned to the next entry.

"I am reminded of Christmas Eve, the night of anticipation. St. Nicholas might be coming, or he might not. Children are always at the mercy of their parents. Children must be good, if there are to be presents. I used to think that parents enjoyed torturing their children. It was as if they wanted their children to worry and pray that some imaginary being would grant their wishes. Parents can be so cruel. I remember there were times when I was terribly disappointed. Will I be disappointed this year? I pray not. I pray."

Hope knew the entry could apply to anything. Haley June could have been talking about the crop in the field or rain on the horizon or any of a million little things. Was she talking about the death of Max? Was she praying that he might die and grant her wish? Yet, Haley June had not mentioned death or Max or anything. She talked about Christmas and parents and anticipation.

Hope read on. There was no entry for the day of Max's murder and Hope found that odd. If Haley June knew about the murder, wouldn't she write about it? Or, was she too excited to write about it? Or, was she too clever to write about it on the day it occurred. How could she know about the murder unless she was involved? She couldn't have known, so she couldn't have written about it.

Hope moved on to the next entry:

"PL stopped by today. He came to tell me he was going to Charleston. He said there were few possibilities for his skills in Wilmington or anywhere abouts. I begged him to stay, but he would not. He said his life was over in Castle Park. He could not stay on. It was done.

We shared the news of the untimely death of Maximillian Johnson. His passing benefits me in no way. While I am not sorry to see him go, I will say nothing ill about him, lest he decide to stay and become my haunt. If I detested him in life, I would certainly loathe him as a haunt. The world is better with him gone.

I thanked PL for his kind attention to my travails. Now that things have changed, I find myself oddly without feeling. I am the child that has opened all her Christmas presents and finds herself wishing for something more. Contentment may never grace my soul. I must face that. I must find a new goal. I'm certain time will soon fill that empty place in my heart. I shall prevail."

Hope stared at the entry for a full minute before she turned the page. The entry was disturbing, as someone could read it as a thinly veiled confession. Had "PL" killed Max? That might be implied to someone who knew the history between Max and Haley June, yet the entry was far from a smoking gun. It didn't overtly state anything at all about Max's death. "PL" may have been kind to Haley, and that was all it meant.

Hope read several more entries and skimmed

still more. She found only one other reference to Max's death:

"Today, the police questioned me about the death of Maximillian Johnson. I was not surprised, as I have a history with Mr. Johnson. The wags that overheard my discussions with the man, no doubt, informed the police of our animosity. That was to be expected. I was truthful. I did not kill Max. While I might have cheered his demise, I could never bring myself to commit such a heinous crime. They left, satisfied that I had nothing to do with the murder. I suspect they were as satisfied as I am."

Hope nodded at the page which addressed Haley's self-awareness of her status as a suspect. She knew she would be interviewed by the police. She expected it, and she was prepared for it. Did that mean she had something to do with the death? Hope knew that the entry would mean nothing in court; they were only the musings of a woman who had had poor relations with a victim. Another smoke signal that would dissipate under hard review.

The rest of the diary returned to daily trivia, events, and people that had no bearing on Max's death. Hope glanced at her watch and knew she had already spent more hours than she'd planned with the diaries. She carefully returned to the entries she thought might be of importance to Max, and took pics of them with her phone. She knew Max would want to read the posts and form his own opinions. She pushed back from the table and stared at the diaries. She was sure that Haley was not involved with Max's death.

A question arose in her mind. Would Max agree with her assessment? Would it be better if she didn't show Max the entries? Would it be better if she simply said she found nothing that proved Haley June had anything to do with his death? Would it be better to simply allow Max to continue a way of life, ghost life, that seemed to please him? She was torn. She knew she didn't want him to leave. They had formed a friendship she hadn't managed to find with anyone else in Castle Park. He was kind and thoughtful and dependable. He filled a spot in her life that needed filling. The diary entries might satisfy Max that he and Hope were right about who had killed him, and there was nothing more to investigate. Would that encourage him to cross over? Would he decide to leave? Then she would be alone ... again.

Did she have to tell him about the contents of the diaries?

Hope sighed.

She knew she had to tell him. To hide what she had found would be to chain him to the house for the foreseeable future. That wasn't fair, no matter how much she might want him to stay. If he decided to accept that Haley June had nothing to with his death, so be it. Hope never wanted to manipulate Max. She wouldn't start now. She would tell him, because that was the right thing to do.

A teachable moment.

Unfortunately, Cori wasn't there to absorb the lesson. In fact, that lesson would have to wait for another example.

Hope sighed. Cori, too, would certainly miss their ghost.

Would Max decide to stay a little longer?

She didn't have an answer.

Hope returned the diaries to the librarian, who asked if they had been of any help. Hope truthfully said that they were both revealing and obscure.

"People are rarely totally truthful, even in their own diaries," the librarian said. "I've read a great many diaries, and I would say that almost all of them shade the truth to benefit the writer."

"History is written by the winners," Hope quipped.

"Precisely. In Roman times, the historians always

wrote with one eye on the current emperor. If they didn't please him, they might lose their head."

"I'm guessing they developed a talent for writing between the lines."

"Or reverted to satire or symbolism. Works every time."

Outside the library, Hope checked her phone. True to the rules, Cori had reported every hour on the hour. Her texts were terse and varied. It seemed the girls had covered most of the campus.

Hope wanted them to experience what a Saturday on a campus was all about. She wished she'd had the chance to visit a campus on a football Saturday. Not that it would have changed her choice of university. It was just something good to know. Hope was about to send a text, when a new one arrived from Cori. Simple and to the point.

HELP!!!!

5

Hope had her phone to her ear, as she hurried across the campus, and just her luck, the fraternity house was way on the other side. As she walked, she kept Cori talking. It didn't matter about what. Hope couldn't afford to lose contact with the girls. Questions about how they arrived at the fraternity house could be answered later.

The fraternity was easily identified, as music blared onto the street. It was an older, orange brick building in need of a fresh paint on its trim. The walk to the front door was painted with various Greek letters that she once knew. She paid no attention and walked around the house. The backyard was large, filled with several picnic tables, two kegs on ice, and a large number of young men and women in various stages of inebriation. It was a party played out on a hundred campuses across the country most every Saturday. The Rap music blasted from large speakers in the windows and several cornhole contests were in progress. Students vied for attention. Some things never changed.

Hope found Cori framed by two young men who were doing their best to impress her. As Hope arrived, her daughter attempted to stand, but one of the young men put a hand on her shoulder to hold her in place. That was all it took to set off Hope.

"Take your hand off her," Hope told the guy.

The young men regarded her.

"Who are you, and what are you doing here?" one asked.

"I'm her mother. For your information, she's fifteen, which she probably told you. So, unless you want to spend some time in prison, I suggest you move off."

The young men looked from Hope to Cori, and laughed.

"Hey, hey, no harm done, Mom," one of them said. "We were just keeping her company."

"I'm sure." Hope scowled.

Cori stood and stepped to her mother's side.

"Where's Lottie?" Hope asked.

Cori pointed. Across the lawn, Lottie sat at a table between two male students, and from the look on the teen's face, she was scared.

"They separated us," Cori said.

"I can see that. Come on."

Hope led the way to the table, even as one of the students helped Lottie to her feet. To Hope, it seemed the student pulled Lottie out of her seat.

"Whoa there," Hope said. "I think you better let me have her."

The student, who looked more than a little drunk, eyed Hope. "Wait your turn, boomer," the young man said. "Finders, keepers."

"Look, Mister," Hope said, "you are playing with fire. The girl is fifteen, which makes her a minor. And she doesn't look like she's enjoying your attention. Anything you do with her is a crime. Do you really want to deal with that?"

"She wants it. I'll give it to her." The young man slurred his words.

"If you weren't drunk, I'd call the cops. You obviously aren't thinking straight." Hope turned to the other young man. "If you're his friend, get him out of here before he does something he'll regret for the rest of his life."

The second guy spoke to his buddy, "Come on. Let the little witch go. We don't want any trouble."

The young man released Lottie. "Come back when you're older."

Lottie rushed over and grabbed Cori's arm.

"Good choice," Hope said to the drunk. "Remember this when you sober up. Check the age first, and make sure to get someone's consent. Otherwise, you'll get into a heap of trouble." She turned to Cori and Lottie. "Let's get out of here."

Hope purposefully did not talk to the teens on the walk back to the car. She knew that they felt guilty. The longer Hope put off the questions, the more guilty they would feel. That was fine with her. She wanted them to feel as bad as possible about not being careful.

"Who wants to go first?" Hope asked, as they drove away from the campus.

"I suppose that would be me," Cori answered. "Teachable moment?"

"Certainly. What did you learn?"

"Well, I guess I should start at the beginning. We were just walking across the campus. You know, just looking at things, and that's when we heard the music so we headed that way. We met Matt and Bert. I don't think those are their real names. They were heading in the same direction, and they invited us to join the party. We didn't think anything of it. I mean, we weren't going to stay, just look around."

"Go on," Hope told her.

"Well, when we got there, they wanted us to drink, but we said no. We weren't going to do that."

"Good decision. You never know what will happen if someone gives you a drink. Sometimes, you can pour it yourself and still not know."

"Yeah, we figured that. That was when I sent you that message. I'm glad you picked it up."

"You're lucky. I had just finished in the library, and I was able to get the text. Is that when they separated you?"

"Yeah, those other guys came over and sort of pulled Lottie away, and the other ones made sure I stayed where I was."

"I wasn't going to go with them anywhere, Mrs. Herring. I was scared."

"You should have been scared. If you research the disappearance of young girls, you'd discover that many of them had no idea they were with bad people. Once they were separated from friends, they became prey."

"Why do people do that?" Cori asked with a tone of disgust.

"Most of the time, they think they can get away with it," Hope answered. "If they give you some sort of drug, or maybe just a lot of alcohol, it can muddle your brain. Things happen, and you might not remember any of it. If they knew they were going to get in trouble, most of them wouldn't bother."

"They knew we were way too young, didn't they?" Lottie asked.

"And inexperienced. Listen, you're going to make mistakes in life. It happens, and as long as the mistake isn't too bad, you'll be all right. But, you have to learn from your mistakes. You can't afford to make the same mistake over and over."

"Next time, you won't be there to save us?" Cori asked.

"Maybe no one will be there to save you." Hope shook her head. "Centuries ago, you two might be married by now."

"Married?" Cori snorted.

"Women married young. They weren't educated formally. They did learn what they were expected to do, and they worked very hard. Marriages were often arranged by families. Love was not guaranteed. In fact, most couples learned to love one another, which is the opposite of today. In our times, couples fall in love and then marry. So, to guarantee that couples remained pure, they often would be accompanied by a chaperone whenever they were together."

"Chaperones?"

"Exactly. It might be an aunt or uncle or friend of the family that would make sure the couple did not act inappropriately."

"That must have been like spying," Lottie said.

"Every mother wanted their daughters to marry well. There would be courtships, and both men and women were encouraged to find a compatible mate, but it didn't always happen. As divorce was very rare in those days, people married for life. If a lot of marriages started off rocky, most of the time, they got better, especially if there were children. In any case, if a woman reached twenty or twenty-five and was unmarried, she was considered an old maid."

Cori looked at her mother with an expression of disbelief. "You're joking. Twenty-five?"

"Children grew up faster back then. Boys as young as ten went to sea as cabin boys. Girls married or went to work in their teens. Of course, many people died earlier, too. Not all that many people lived to be sixty or seventy. You two should read some history. You'll discover just how pampered we are now."

"We'll learn another lesson, right?" Cori asked.

"A valuable one. Be thankful for what you have and try not to be too stupid."

"I think I'll stay away from colleges for a while," Lottie said.

"Good idea. Now, do we need to tell people about your little adventure?"

"I … I don't think so," Lottie said. "If that's all right with you."

"I'm with Lottie," Cori said. "I think we can keep it to ourselves."

"Then, we'll let it go this time," Hope said. "As long as it doesn't happen again."

"You know," Lottie said, "after what I did with Exotic Kitty, you would think I'd avoid going anywhere with anyone."

"Learn, girls, learn."

If the girls heard, they didn't show it. Hope noted that they had devolved into tapping on their phones. She wondered if their little fracas at the fraternity would be posted on a social network platform. How many "likes" would it earn? Popularity was the name of the game.

The drive home was silent. Hope didn't suggest stopping for food, as that seemed like some sort of reward for their lax behavior. Hope's father had always told her that everything he did for her was a reward. If she did positive things, he rewarded her in a positive way. He rewarded her according to her behavior. She liked to think she did the same with Cori. Good behavior resulted in good rewards. Simple and to the point. So, no stopping for a burger, no banter, no levity. They had not behaved in a safe manner.

"Did you post?" Hope asked her daughter after Lottie had left the car, and they'd driven home.

"No," Cori answered. "But I think Lottie did. Not the whole story, just hints, you know? She just wants the others to ask about it. She'll make it sound dramatic, like she was about to be attacked or something. Lottie likes attention."

"We all do. We're social animals. We like people to acknowledge us."

"Yeah, well, sometimes, attention can be bad," Cori admitted.

"I know. When you've done something really dumb, you don't want a spotlight on you, right?"

Cori shrugged. "That only makes it worse."

"I can't give you a lot of advice there. How much attention is enough? How much is too much? I don't know. That's one of those pendulum areas."

"Pendulum?"

"Some things swing back and forth, like a pendulum. Things go in one direction for a while, until they meet some sort of peak. Then, they swing in the other direction. For some moment, perhaps longer than a moment, the pendulum is perfectly vertical, in balance. Then, it sweeps in the other direction."

"Until it reaches another stopping point?"

"Exactly. Attention can be like that. You get some, and you get more, and you think everything is perfect. But the pendulum doesn't stop there. It keeps going, and the extra attention is no fun at all."

"That's how school is. I think everything is just fine," Cori said, "then, someone says something or does something, and everything goes to ashes."

"I suppose that's how life is. You're happy one day, sad the next, and then happy again after that. Good weeks and bad weeks. Spring always follows winter."

"You sound like a guidance counselor."

"Sometimes, you dig yourself into a hole, and you don't think you'll ever climb out. But, you will, eventually. Then, you'll soar like an eagle. That won't last either. Gravity will pull you back to earth. I guess you can say gravity works on the pendulum, too. Swing too far, and gravity works its magic. But overall, we get more good days than bad."

"I know we didn't stop for dinner because you didn't want us to think that we did something worth celebrating."

"Well, you were smart enough to call me, and you didn't let Lottie out of your sight. So, that was good. You handled it well. What do you say we go out and eat Chinese food?"

"Works for me. I think it should be just the two of us."

"And, we won't talk about teachable moments," Hope told her.

"Roger that."

"Why don't you go to your room and freshen up. I have to check my email before we go."

Hope trudged up the steps to her office, and there, she found Max, reading something on the screen.

"Hello, Mrs. Herring. I have discovered that there are cameras everywhere. I am looking at one in Sydney, Australia. Fascinating."

"Yes, it's fun to see what the cameras show. We just got back from the university. I have some news."

Max turned, smiling, as he always did.

"I read Haley June's diaries, well, some of them. I took pics of the sections that I thought you should read. I'm going to email them to you. Read them while Cori and I are at dinner. We can discuss it when I get back."

"No hints, Mrs. Herring?"

"No, Max, I don't wish to influence your opinion."

"That's fair. I shall read them and cogitate on them until you return. No matter what they say, I must thank you for the hard work."

"I hope they help, Max. I really do."

6

When she returned from the restaurant, Hope didn't find Max in the office. She considered calling out to him, but that might appear to be a summons of some sort. She guessed he was still processing the information she had brought back from Chapel Hill. If he was, she didn't wish to disturb him. He would know best how to interpret Haley June's diary. If he wanted Hope's input, he would ask for it. She read and answered some email, and then decided it was time for bed.

She checked on Cori, who, for once, was not on her phone. The teen was playing a game of chess on her computer.

"Winning?" Hope asked.

"No. I lost a knight early, and I can't seem to get

back to even. It's just a matter of time, unless the computer makes a blunder."

"Will that happen?"

Cori shook her head. "The computer doesn't make a blunder very often, unless you're playing it on 'easy' mode."

"So, you're fighting a losing battle?"

"I am, but that's part of learning. You never know when you can capture something and even the game."

"Sounds like war."

"It is, but it's civilized war," Cori said. "I'll tell you this, you never want to be a pawn. Those guys get wiped out early."

"Well, get some sleep. Tomorrow, we'll go to that Christmas tree farm and select a tree for the holiday."

"Great. Can Lottie go with us? If I go out there without her, she'll think I'm making a move on River."

"And, Lottie wants to make a move on him herself, right?"

"You know Lottie."

"I do. Sure, she can come if her mom says it's all right. If her mother wants to go with us, that would be fine, too. She can pick out a tree for their house."

"I'll text Lottie. Thanks, Mom."

"Good luck with the war."

Cori chuckled. "Luckily, it's not a real war. I'd become a POW in a minute."

"Then it's a good thing it's not a real war. Sleep in fifteen minutes?"

Cori smiled. "Sure. I'll have lost the game by then."

∽

In her bedroom, Hope's thoughts turned again to Max. It was difficult for her to just let him alone. They had become good friends, and good friends did not let friends suffer. She guessed the diary entries had kindled any number of memories, any number of explanations, any number of ideas as to his murder. She couldn't blame Max for retreating into a contemplative shell. He had waited for a century to determine who had killed him. Why would he hurry now? Hope fell asleep, wondering when he would emerge from his analysis.

At breakfast, Hope found out that Adele would join them for the Christmas tree trek. All morning, Hope waited for Max to make an appearance, but he never did, and a small worry took root in her brain.

Was he satisfied that he knew who had killed him, and so moved on?

No, he would never leave without telling her. That would be wrong, and Max would never do that. Hope decided that Max was like the butterfly in the cocoon. He would come out when the time was right.

"I hope this place has good trees," Adele said.

Hope consulted the GPS on her dash. "I'm sure they do. Luckily, it's not too far away. I never knew there was a tree farm so close."

"Yeah, most of them are in the mountains out west. That's a good four hours from here. Do you know how this place is going to tag the tree you pick out? I mean, how can we make sure we get the tree we ordered?"

"Honesty, I suppose. I mean, we can watch them tag the tree, but tags can be swapped, right? Your tree today could be someone else's tree tomorrow."

"You think they can sell that perfect tree over and over?" Adele looked displeased with the possibility.

"I don't think so, but hey, who knows."

"If they did that sort of thing, they wouldn't be in business for very long." Adele looked out the window. "Lottie told me about the fraternity party."

"I was pretty sure she would."

"Was it as dramatic as she made it sound?"

"It hadn't reached that stage yet, although the young men who were with Lottie were drunk enough to try something very stupid."

"I'm glad you and Cori were there."

"They weren't supposed to go to any fraternities or sororities, but you know temptation. I'm guessing they thought they could go for a few minutes and then leave ... and never tell us."

Adele laughed. "That's what I would have done, but I might have stayed longer than just a few minutes."

"I like to think they learned something, but that doesn't always happen. It seems that most of us keep falling into the same old patterns."

"We do. It's hard not to slip into those old patterns of behavior."

The gate to Soames Tree Farm was at the end of a dirt road in need of a serious grading. Hope was reduced to crawling along, trying to avoid the holes that threatened her car's suspension.

"I'm glad we're not doing this at night," Adele said. "We'd be bouncing all over the place."

The house and barn were three quarters of a mile past the gate. Christmas trees lined both sides of the lane, neat rows of green trees that looked to be just right for cutting. Beyond them, Hope noticed some plots with trees only two or three feet high. That made her wonder about how old a tree had to be before it was harvested. No doubt, a good tree farm would have to plant crop after crop, so that they always had a good supply of trees.

Several cars were in the large, dirt parking lot. Hope pulled her SUV into a spot, and everyone piled out.

There was a large farmhouse ahead that was showing its years. The house needed painting and new gutters, and the long porch across the front sagged in the middle, telling Hope that it needed new underpinnings. Set to one side was a big, red barn, which looked newer and in better shape than the house.

Hope wondered if there were pigs or cows on the farm. She didn't think so, but the barn would house whatever insecticides, pesticides, and fertilizers the trees required. She knew there were always insects with a hunger for trees.

As they approached the barn, a man stepped out and Hope recognized him as the man who had been in the restaurant with River the other evening. He grinned at them.

"Welcome to Soames Farm," he said. "Here to pick out a tree?"

"We think so," Adele said. "Can you tell us how this works?"

"Sure, it's not complicated. You pick out the tree, and then we tag it with an electronic unit, a little transponder that's picked up by our readers. We have a web page where you can locate the trees and check on it. Sorry, our cameras aren't always sophisticated enough to locate individual trees, but you'll be able to see the entire plot. You can check on your tree at any time. Your tag won't change. When you're ready for your tree, send us an email, text, or call. We'll cut the tree, bundle it, and deliver it to your vehicle right here. We'll tie it down, and you drive off. Someday, we hope to be able to deliver trees, but right now, you have to pick them up."

Hope noted how easy the man was with the explanation. No doubt he had said the same thing many times. She noted the leather sheaf that held a large knife, the worn work boots, and leather gloves tucked into the back pocket of his jeans.

"Sounds very efficient," Adele said. "Can we come out and visit our tree?"

"During normal working hours and as long as we're not spraying or cutting. We adhere to all environmental laws and regulations, so there are times when you can't be here."

Hope spotted Lottie and Cori looking around. She guessed they were trying to find River. If he wasn't a member of the Soames family, the girls probably would have stayed at home.

A loud engine drew Hope's attention, and she turned to see a large, multicolored bus limp into the parking lot. It had been a school bus at one time, but now, it was some kind of rainbow vehicle, belching dark smoke as steam escaped from under the hood. In the middle of the parking lot, the bus simply stopped. The engine died, and for a moment, nothing happened. Then, the door opened, and half a dozen people hopped out.

To Hope, the group looked like throwbacks to a different era. Long hair and beards on the men, long hair and no bras on the women. They were like the hippies from the past. She guessed they were part of the "free spirit" crowd that always traveled in torn jeans, dirty T-shirts, and broad smiles. People looking for something better than what they had, believing that Utopia could be attained, if only the right people came together.

The last person off the bus was younger than the others, eighteen or nineteen by Hope's guess. What set her off from the others was ... her beauty. It was that simple. Blond, high cheek bones, red lips, a svelte body that might have belonged to an athlete or a dancer, her physical appearance caused everyone to look at her, including Cori and Lottie. The girl could have been a movie star or model. She was that attractive. She looked around and smiled.

"River!" the tree farmer yelled.

From the barn, out strolled River as handsome as ever. Sweaty, in jeans and a tee, he joined his father.

"What's up?"

"Take these folks to the plot and show them the trees for sale. I got to talk to my cousin."

River looked at the bus, and Hope noticed a change in the boy's face. He stared at the blonde, completely enthralled for the moment. Hope didn't blame him. The blonde was worth looking at.

"Get going," the dad said. "Remember to take a couple of tags."

River tore his eyes from the blonde long enough to look at Adele and Hope. "I'll be right back."

Hope watched the farmer march over to the newly arrived group. She couldn't hear what was being said, but she could tell that not everything was hunky-dory. She guessed that the group was unexpected. The bus women headed for the farmhouse, probably for a potty break. The men talked and pointed. It was obvious that the bus had developed some sort of problem that would require a repair.

River returned with two small boxes. He looked at the group, but since the blonde wasn't there, he turned to Hope and Adele.

"Follow me." He started to the left rows of trees.

Cori and Lottie fell into step with River. They started a conversation of sorts. Hope didn't listen. She didn't want to know too much so she and Adele lagged behind.

"They're growing up fast, aren't they?" Adele asked.

"It's inevitable," Hope replied. "Sometimes, I wish I could park Cori in some school someplace and tell them I'll come back for her in ten years."

"I hear you. I don't look forward to what's coming. Lottie has always been more difficult than Cori. I don't expect that to change. Think we have to worry about River?"

"Not as long as that blond girl is around. He seemed pretty fixated on her."

"I noticed, and I saw why," Adele said. "She's gorgeous. It's not just because she's young. If I sound envious, it's because I am."

Hope laughed. "She'll soon know what we know.

Those looks won't last forever, and there's nothing anyone can do about it."

"Sometimes, I think we put too much emphasis on beauty. I mean, it's in the eye of the beholder, right?"

Hope shared, "Actually, I read where they did a study, and it showed that people pretty much pick the same pretty people, no matter what. When people are being rated as better looking or not better looking, for the most part, the raters all sort the people the same way. Seems humans share the same idea of what beauty looks like."

"I suppose you're right. Otherwise, why would you see the same faces on different magazine covers? We all know a handsome or pretty face when we see it."

"Are you going to pick a tree today?" Hope asked.

"I don't see why not. I mean, it's a pretty good deal. Since we can watch it online, we can be sure they're not switching trees on us."

"Gives me a warm feeling … and saves a lot of looking."

Ahead, the girls matched River's pace. To Hope, it was a sign of times to come.

7

Hope found the walk surprisingly warm, as there didn't seem to be a lot of breeze amidst the trees. They walked up one row of well-groomed trees, all in the conical shape that was the mark of a good Christmas tree.

"Do you think they grow this way naturally?" Adele asked.

"No," Hope answered. "I'm sure there's some pruning and shaping to be done. They're selling Christmas trees, so they have to look good."

"Yeah, these are too perfect to be untouched. They all look great, don't they?"

Hope chuckled. "You just have to choose the one that will fit inside your house."

"How much do you think they'll lop off when they cut down a tree?"

"We'll have to ask, but I imagine you can specify. Tell them you want a seven-foot tree, and they'll cut it to fit."

"I suppose you're right. So, start with an eight-footer and work down?"

"You'll want them to cut some off the bottom before you put it in water, too. The tree will draw better that way."

"I know that." Adele turned to watch Cori and Lottie. "The girls are a little infatuated, aren't they?"

"I guess they're making that first foray into being attracted to a boy. They know we're here, so they can't act too flirty, or get in any trouble. Time to test themselves, I guess."

"I still remember being that way when I had a crush on Jeremy Thompson. He was good looking and played basketball. When we got a couple of years older, he didn't pay much attention to me, but I worshipped him from afar. When I did get a chance to talk to him, I might as well have been a monkey. I jabbered on and made no sense." Adele laughed. "I guess, sometimes, I still act like a schoolgirl."

"Crushes were the thing," Hope recalled. "Every girl in school had a crush on someone. Might be an athlete or a teacher. I had a science teacher who was handsome and smart. Luckily, he was happily married with kids."

"Mistake avoided is a good thing."

"Absolutely." Hope walked around the groupings of trees. "We need to choose a tree."

"It's hard. They all look good."

Hope and Adele caught up with the girls, and ten minutes later, they had picked out trees. Hope watched as River wrote down the tag number and the access code on a pad.

"Once you're on the app, you can use the code to access the grid and find your tree. You can check on it as often as you like. There are cameras, but they're kind of fuzzy. Sometimes the tags fail. If that happens, call us, and we'll retag it."

He tore sheets off the pad and handed them over.

"So, when we want the tree, we just call?" Adele asked.

"Or use the app. You can make a time to pick it up. We'll make sure it's ready."

"I guess we have no excuses this year, do we?" Hope said. "Pick up the tree and trim it before the day is out."

"We have tree stands, if you need one," River told them.

"I don't need one. I'm good with the one I have," Adele said.

"I think we might need a new one," Lottie offered.

"We'll see."

The walk back to the barn was mostly in silence. Hope couldn't help but remember that she hadn't seen Max for a while. She understood why, but it did bother her a little. He needed time and space. She would give him that. She hoped she hadn't sent him into some sort of depression.

In the barn, Hope paid for the tree while River loaded the app on everyone's phones. Hope wondered if Cori and Lottie would be using the phone to survey the tree and, maybe, catch a snowy glimpse of River moving up and down the rows. She guessed that little spy game wouldn't last long, as the odds of spotting River were small. The girls would soon learn that it would be far easier to shadow him in school.

Once the phones were loaded and operational, Hope knew it was time to go. Other customers had arrived, and they were walking among the trees. When River nodded and headed off to help the new customers, disappointment clouded the girls' faces.

"Hey," Hope said. "Where are we going for lunch?"

"It's past lunchtime," Cori said.

"Then, we'll call it an early supper. Who's up for catfish?" Hope asked playfully.

"Yuck," Lottie said.

"Don't listen to my mom," Cori said. "She doesn't like catfish either. She just wants us to offer something better."

"I vote for Andy's," Adele said. "Good burgers, a salad bar, great shakes."

"Works for me," Hope said.

The girls agreed.

As they walked to the vehicle, Hope noticed that the rainbow bus was still parked where it had died. The group had moved to a small, empty field next to the house where they were busy setting up tents for a camp. There were too many of them to stay in the house—unless it rained. They could use the facilities and still sleep outdoors. To Hope, the camp meant the hippies were going to be at the farm for a while. The blond girl pulled a support cord tight and tied it to a peg in the ground. She moved with a grace that made Hope think she'd had some dance training. She had that sort of poise.

"Can they just set up their tents and stay here?" Cori asked.

"If they have the owner's permission," Hope answered. "Camping is probably better than squeezing them into the house."

"Can't they stay on the bus?" Lottie asked.

"The bus will likely get very hot and uncomfortable," Adele said. "They'll bake inside. No breeze."

Inside the SUV, the girls checked the new app and their trees. As advertised, they could find their tagged trees. Little red dots marked the spots. The new toy would keep them occupied for a little while, but only for a little while.

Andy's restaurant was crowded, but it was a popular spot for families. Good food, quick service, reasonable prices, it provided everything a family was looking for. Hope forced herself to engage with the others. She would be home before long, and she would find Max soon enough. And then she would learn his thoughts and decisions.

"This is so cool," Lottie said. "Our very own Christmas tree is on my phone."

Hope smiled. Lottie was doing exactly what the tree farmers wanted. She was sharing the acquisition of the tree. Hope guessed that the tree farm would go viral before long. More and more people would think it was cool to tag their own tree. It might become the hit of the season.

Once home, Cori disappeared into her room, no doubt to share the tree shopping experience with her friends, and Hope headed for her attic office. She expected to find Max there, and she wasn't disappointed. He was wearing his funeral suit and playing a game of Sudoku on the computer.

"Hello, Max."

"Mrs. Herring, I have become addicted to this ingenious game. When I first happened upon it, I thought it was about numbers, but, it's not. It's all about logic. Any nine unique symbols will do. Quite sporting."

"It is. There are certain techniques you can apply to the puzzle, which helps. They're all online, probably."

"They are, and I have learned a few. However, I am afraid I will never achieve professional status. My brain was not built for such a puzzle."

Hope looked at him for a moment. "I suppose we should discuss the diaries?"

"Indeed, Mrs. Herring, we must." Max turned away from the screen and smiled. "You have achieved the impossible. A one-hundred-year-old murder has been solved. I don't believe even Sherlock Holmes might have achieved that."

"I don't think the diary entries are definitive. Haley doesn't say she killed you, or that she knows who killed you."

"I know that, and it is because we were right in the first place. Davis Ellison and his sister Margaret are guilty of my murder, not Haley."

"You're not suspicious of PL?"

"Preston Lee Conrad. Haley always called him Preston Lee, which is the "PL" in her diary. He was devoted to her, but I do not think the man was a killer. I also do not believe Haley was capable of murder. She was full of hate, but I do not believe she could commit the act. I suppose I knew that in the back of my mind. I just needed to be sure."

"You're no fool, Max. And, if you're not completely satisfied, I can continue the investigation."

"That will not be necessary. I am not an idiot. We have achieved what I set out to do. That brings my quest to an end. It allows me to leave the house and move on."

Hope's heart dropped. "Maybe you shouldn't be hasty about it. Take the time to fully digest what you've learned."

"Mrs. Herring, I appreciate your caution, but I am quite certain I am right. Haley June did not kill me, and neither did her brother. It is that simple."

Hope nodded, a great sadness in her heart. "Are you thinking of leaving soon?"

"No, I will not hurry away, but I suppose it will be time for me to go fairly soon."

"I know you set a goal, so that you could move on. That's reasonable, but you have not, in any fashion, exhausted the knowledge you might discover if you stay. I don't mean about your murder. I mean about the world."

Max smiled. "I doubt that knowledge will keep in good stead on the other side."

"You're probably right. Well, will you stay just a bit longer for me and Cori?"

Max's eyes widened. "You still want me to stay on?"

"Yes, Max, I want you to stay on. I don't know how you view our relationship, but I have found it a wonderful friendship. You have protected the house and us, and you've made my life far more satisfying than I thought it would be when I moved here."

"I shall think about it, Mrs. Herring. In the natural order of things, I'm already late to the dance, if you know what I mean."

"I do, and since you're already late, might you keep us company for a bit longer? That's selfish on my part, and if it's too much to ask, then, of course you must go."

"I don't know what I will face once I leave. I doubt that it will be much better than what I have here. I thoroughly enjoy being here with you, and I enjoy Cori and our chats."

"And she enjoys her chats with you, too, as do I. I know you want to see your wife and daughter on the other side so don't stay if you feel it's time to go."

"That is very kind of you, Mrs. Herring. For a ghost, the passing of time is but a moment. It does not feel like I have lingered for a hundred years. If you are willing to put up with my staying on, then I will have to give it serious consideration."

He laughed, and she laughed with him.

"If you like being here, we would love to have you stay."

Max smiled. "Mrs. Herring, that is very kind of you. I will ponder it for a little while."

8

By Wednesday, Max had still not communicated his plans, but Hope didn't press. The ghost was entitled to all the time he needed. She knew the choice was not an easy one to make. It was one thing to die unexpectedly, it was quite another to choose the afterlife over living as a ghost. She was confident that he would decide soon. Then, it would be matter of adjustment. She told herself that moving on would be the logical choice for Max. That would sadden her, but she vowed to deal with the loss the best she could.

"How is our tree doing?" Hope asked as Cori walked over to the SUV where it was parked in the lot of her school.

"Just fine," Cori answered. "How did you know I checked on it?"

"It's something new to do. The routineness of checking hasn't started yet. I don't know if there's a study to show how long the excitement of newness lasts."

"Excitement of newness?"

"Most people love to get gifts. They love the frenzy of opening packages and pulling out something new. That good feeling lasts for a while. Then, the magic of the bright, new shiny bauble wears off. There's no way to restart it, so people buy the next, new, shiny bauble."

"Is that why some people keep buying shoes?" Cori questioned. "Lottie's mother has at least a hundred pairs of shoes. It seems there's always a new box on the kitchen counter."

"Shoes are a favorite of some people. It's especially easy, because they can shop online. They find the shoes at a great price, and they convince themselves they need them. Of course, the magic dissipates after a while, and they start all over again. Buying shoes online is much easier than going to an old-fashioned shoe store."

"How come you don't buy shoes?"

"I do. I just limit myself to buying what I need.

That's the first question I ask myself. Do I need another pair of shoes?"

"I guess you don't because you don't own that many."

"I already own several pairs I haven't worn in a year," Hope explained. "I suppose I should get rid of them. Otherwise, they'll just rot away in the closet."

"If I got a new pair of shoes, I'd wear them all the time."

"Until they no longer gave you that endorphin rush."

Cori shrugged. "Roger that." The teen spotted River waiting on the sidewalk. "I think he needs a ride."

"What makes you say that?" Hope questioned.

"He always takes the bus. So, if he missed his bus, he's waiting for someone."

"Do you think we should ask if we can drop him somewhere?"

Cori beamed. "Sure, I'll ask him."

Hope watched as Cori hustled over to River, and after a very brief exchange, both of them came back to the vehicle.

"He needs a ride," Cori said.

"Miss the bus?" Hope asked.

"My dad was supposed to pick me up. I guess he got busy, or he forgot."

"Well, before we leave, text him and tell him you have a ride. We don't want him to arrive and find you missing."

"Yes, Mrs. Herring, I'll make sure he doesn't come for me."

Cori and River sat in the back as Hope drove out to the tree farm. She couldn't help but overhear the conversation.

"I've been watching my tree," Cori said. "It's cool."

"Yeah," River answered. "Watching the trees is getting more popular as word spreads about it across the net. I think people like the idea of not having much to do when it's time to put up a Christmas tree."

"That's a good thing."

River frowned. "It might be better if we didn't have the magic bus around."

"Magic bus?"

"That's what Dad calls it. You probably don't know, but the bus driver is my dad's brother. Dad never talks much about him. I guess, Uncle Pete doesn't like to work much. He and those other people just drive around the country, living on what they can beg for or steal. That's what Dad says anyway. They live on food stamps."

"Why are they still around?" Cori asked.

"The magic bus needs some work. Uncle Pete doesn't have the money, and Dad doesn't either. I heard them arguing about it. Dad told Uncle Pete to get a job, and that made Uncle Pete shout something about dad being a tree killer. We don't kill trees. We grow them."

"Do you know when they're leaving?"

"No, no one does. Lauren says they won't stay long."

"Lauren?"

"Oh, yeah, she's the blond girl. She's really nice."

Hope noticed the change in River's voice when he talked about Lauren. It was clear that River liked her. Hope wanted to tell him that Lauren was a bit too old for him, but she guessed he would learn that as soon as the magic bus moved on down the road.

"What about the others?" Cori asked. "Aren't they going to leave even if the bus doesn't?"

"Well, I don't know. Sky doesn't talk to me. She sort of grunts when she wants something. It's weird. She'll talk to the others, but I guess I don't qualify or something. Sky and Lauren don't get along all that well. I don't get it because Lauren is so nice. There's

Conair, too. He's not as weird as Sky, but he's dangerous. He has all these tattoos, all over his arms and body. Dad says I should stay away from Conair because he's drunk or high all the time. The other night he was running through the trees, and he was naked. He was yelling something about a blood moon."

Cori's eyes widened. "Sounds like quite a group."

"Yeah. They're headed for California. They said that's the place for them, free spirits and all."

"I guess you'll be happy to see them leave."

"Most of them. Mom doesn't like any of them. She keeps telling Dad he should just kick them out."

"That's probably not a bad idea," Cori admitted.

"I think they have guns on the bus. I mean, I haven't seen any, but Dad says Uncle Pete likes guns. He always has some around."

Cori made a face. "You have to be careful around guns."

"I know."

Hope stopped listening at that point as both River and Cori went to their phones. She could only guess what they were texting. She was certain Cori was telling Lottie that River was in the car. River was probably doing something else, perhaps looking up sports scores.

She turned into the parking lot of the tree farm and saw the magic bus was where it had stopped. There appeared to be no activity even remotely related to repair, and the tents still graced the field. Sky, Conair, and Uncle Pete sat in folding chairs smoking cigarettes. Lauren emerged from the shadows inside the barn. She did not look happy.

"I thought there were six on the bus," Hope said.

"Two left already. I guess they didn't want to hang around," River answered.

"Here you are," Hope told River as she pulled to a stop.

"Thanks for the ride, Mrs. Herring. I appreciate it. I guess Dad forgot about me."

"Any time," Cori said. "We're happy to bring you home."

When River climbed out of the vehicle, Hope watched as he said something to Lauren, who shrugged and kept walking. River frowned and headed for the barn, even as his father walked out. If there were going to be words between them, Hope didn't want to hear them. She turned around and drove out.

"Do you like him?" Cori asked.

"Who?"

"You playing an owl now? You know who ... River."

"I don't know him well enough to have an opinion," Hope said.

"That's a bogus cop out."

"No, it's the truth. I'll put it to you this way. Have you ever gone online to look for a hotel room? You know, to find a place that's both nice and cheap?"

"You know I have. I help you with that all the time."

"And, you know that how it looks online is the best it's ever going to look, right? They're showing you the very nicest of everything."

"Well, duh, of course, I know that."

"It's the same with people. That online photo is the best one they can find. In most cases, it's years younger than what those people actually are. Sure, they looked like that once, but that's not how they look today. You know that the pic is as good as it gets. If you don't like the pic, you won't like them."

"Your point?"

"When River is in the car with us, he's on his best behavior. He's not going to be suddenly more concerned or attentive. He's not going to be smarter. He's not going to be more engaging. To think that is to live in a fantasyland. So, while I've seen River at his best, I don't know what he might be like on an everyday basis. That won't be revealed to me until he becomes comfortable enough to let his true self shine through."

"You make him sound like some sort of psycho manipulator."

"Human nature. We all want to make a good first impression."

"Yeah, you're right. I see it all the time with other girls. They're all as sweet as sugar at first, then, sometimes things sour."

"Sometimes, people are like restaurant menus."

"What?" Cori chuckled.

"They look yummy and enticing until you realize that the photos on the menu aren't of actual meals. They're carefully orchestrated views of often nonedible and touched-up stuff. A good photographer can make a dish look like something that will make our mouths water. But, it's an exaggeration."

"Roger that. I get you. No one scrubs the floor in their prom dress."

"Roger that."

Cori laughed. "So I should keep an eye on River?"

"Might be a good idea."

At home, Hope climbed the steps up to her

office, and there, she found Max at the computer wearing jodhpur's, black riding boots, and a white shirt. With slicked dark hair, he looked as if he had stepped out of some movie about the very rich.

"Going horseback riding?" Hope asked.

"No, just surfing a bit, learning more about how to make movies. There are a great many articles and books dedicated to film. There is far more technique and art involved than I originally thought."

"The art of film is to keep the audience glued to their seats. If they don't become engaged with what's on the screen, the movie will be a flop," Hope said.

"I agree. That must be one reason why they keep cinemas dark and quiet. With lights on and people chatting, you can't very well fall into the world in front of you."

Hope asked, "Does this mean you're not going to slip away?"

He smiled. "It certainly does, Mrs. Herring. I have decided that I can hardly do better in the next realm than I am doing here. Now that the anxiety of my murder had been eased, I find myself enjoying what comes my way. Sometime in the future, I will decide to cross. When that happens, I will inform you, but for now, I very much enjoy your and Cori's company."

"I'm very glad you're staying on, Max. I know that someday, you'll leave, but I'm glad that day hasn't arrived yet. Of course, there may come a day when I'll leave this house. I won't do that without consulting with you, but life doesn't guarantee much."

"I am well aware of that. I will tell you now, that if you leave, I will leave as well. I know I shall never find a better owner than you, or a better friend."

"Never say never. I'm sure you're capable of charming whoever might buy this old place." Hope smiled.

"You overestimate my skills, Mrs. Herring. I was always, and I remain, a simple man with simple goals. If I have any charm, it is in my honesty, which I have worked on religiously. I hope that doesn't sound like bragging."

"It doesn't. Honor is not a well-taught topic in today's world. It seems people are more concerned about their things than their sacred honor."

Max nodded. "Indeed, I have found that obvious online."

"We'll table honor for the moment, as we can't speak for everyone. And I agree with what you said … I couldn't ask for a better friend than you."

9

On Friday, Hope, Cori, Lottie, and Adele went to the Pizza Corner for a delicious Italian dinner. The work week was over and it was time to relax, and they'd come early to beat the crowds. While Hope and Adele chatted over glasses of red wine, the girls were eyes down on their phones. Hope didn't scold them ... not right away at least. In a few minutes, she would remind them that they were responsible for polite conversation and that phone texts could wait.

"Have you thought about what you're going to do for Halloween?" Adele asked.

"It's still September." Hope smiled at her friend. "I refuse to think about candy and costumes until at least October fifteenth."

"I'm thinking of having a costume party. Don't

you think that would be an absolute blast? We'll put the kids in the basement while the adults bob for apples or whatever we want to do."

"That's fine, but you can't have a party on Halloween. Trick-or-treaters need their sugar fix."

"I was thinking about the weekend before. Not too big a party, just enough people to ensure a good time. Oh, and we can give out prizes for the best costumes. Don't you think that would be fun?"

"It would. I'll help you with it. Just tell me what to do."

"I'll let you know. Oh, you can bake us a great Halloween cake. You know, black cake, black icing, pics of vampires and spiders and witches."

"I can do that. You're going to turn the house into something haunted, aren't you?"

"I am. I wonder if I can rent a ghost for the evening."

Hope's face almost went white. "A ghost?"

"Not a real ghost, although that would be wicked cool. A fake ghost that will pop out from behind the sofa and scare people."

"A ghost for hire?" Hope relaxed. "I'm guessing you can find one online. You can find everything else online."

At that moment, the group from the tree farm entered the restaurant. Sky, Uncle Pete, Conair, and last in line ... Lauren, and she wasn't smiling. She wore a T-shirt that said 'Goodbye, did you say something?"

The group found a table not far from where Hope, Adele, and the girls were sitting. The foursome was loud as they plopped into their seats and called for drinks. Hope sensed that Lauren was not comfortable. Something seemed wrong.

"What are they doing here?" Adele asked, annoyed with their behavior.

"Best Italian food in town." Hope shrugged.

"I know, but they're roadies, right? I mean, they look like they need a washing and a shave."

Hope laughed. "I'm sure they'll be just fine. They're like bikers ... beards, leather, and hard lines, but they're generally not all that bad."

"Not unless they come in gangs."

Hope took the moment to chide the girls into putting down their phones. Lottie held up one finger and did a few quick taps on her phone.

"Bummer," Lottie said.

"What is it?" Adele asked.

"Our tree went dead."

"Tree? What tree?"

"The Christmas tree. I can't get a signal. The whatever it is went dead."

Lottie showed her phone to Adele, who frowned. "That's not supposed to happen."

"You don't think someone took our tree, do you?" Lottie asked.

"I'm sure it's just some kind of glitch." Adele looked at Cori. "Did you check your tree?"

"I'll see if the system is up," Cori offered. She tapped her phone a few times. "Our tree is still beeping. Must be the tag on the tree."

Adele pulled out her phone. "I'm going to call them right now. I don't want someone else to get our tree."

"It can wait, Adele. I doubt that there's anything to be done tonight. Call in the morning. Go out there, if you need to. Make sure your tree is still there. But I don't think it will come to that. Once they retag it, you can compare it to where it was before."

"You're right, Hope. I'm not going to the farm tonight. If I wander out into the trees, the mosquitoes will eat me alive. They sneak out at dusk."

The waitress arrived, and they ordered their meals, and as they did, Conair at the other table whooped about something. Hope didn't look over since that was probably what he wanted. She guessed he was someone who craved attention. That was the reason for all the tattoos. He wanted people to look at him.

And, Cori and Lottie did look.

"Turn around," Hope told the girls. "He's doing it so you'll look, which is what he wants. Ignore him, and he'll stop."

But, Conair didn't stop. He whooped and shouted and, generally, made a nuisance of himself. Hope glanced over and found Lauren trying to tame him. As she watched, Conair reached out and grabbed Lauren's blond hair. Lauren yelped, and Uncle Pete stood. He punched Conair in the side of the head, knocking him over.

"Get out," Uncle Pete told Conair. "Get out, before I do something I'll regret later."

Conair rubbed his head. "You got no cause to ambush me like that."

"I put up with a lot of your crap, Conair. But, you never touch the women, hear? You know that. Now, go! Get out."

Conair got to his feet. "I won't forget this, Pete. No sir, I won't forget. I'm gonna let this one go, cause you're right ... I shouldn't have grabbed her hair, but next time, I'll make you pay."

"Find yourself another ride home," Uncle Pete said. "And, if you don't make it back, that's fine by me. I'm getting tired of your B.S."

Conair's face wrinkled into an evil sneer. "You talk big, but you won't be so big when I'm through with you."

With that, Conair headed out. Uncle Pete watched till the young man was gone before he turned to Lauren.

"He hurt you?"

Lauren shook her head. "I won't say I don't appreciate what you did, but I could have handled him myself."

"I know, but if I let you two fight, then we'd all get kicked out. I'm hungry and I don't want to miss out on some good food."

"You better watch your six," Sky said to Uncle Pete. "Conair has a mean streak, and he doesn't like to come at people head on, if you know what I mean."

"Let's just forget about Conair. I'll lay even odds that he don't come back to the bus tonight."

"There," Lottie said.

Hope turned to the girls. "What?"

"I used the app and sent a message to River. I

told him that we couldn't communicate with our tree."

"Great," Adele said. "Let me know if he answers."

"I will."

Hope looked around, but the fireworks were over. She spotted the owner standing to one side, quietly surveying the magic bus group. With Conair gone, they seemed subdued. She knew that more than one group discovered that some members weren't good for cohesion. Conair was a disruptive force. That might be welcome, if the group needed to challenge someone else. A man like Conair couldn't stop himself. He needed the chaos. He would rile his own friends, if all else failed.

Hope and Adele chatted until the food arrived. Then, everyone was too busy eating to talk, and that was when Lauren arrived next to their table.

"I want to apologize," Lauren said. "Things got a little out of hand."

"It's all right," Adele said. "No harm done to anyone, I hope. And, he's gone."

"Yeah, he's gone. We probably never should have brought him here in the first place. Conair isn't known for his manners."

"Is your bus repaired?" Hope asked.

"That's right, you were out there the other day. You bought a tree, right?"

"We did, a very good tree."

"Oh, and you brought River home the other day, too. That was generous of you."

"Nothing to it. So, you don't know how long you're going to be staying at the tree farm?" Hope asked.

"Pete says we're waiting for a part. Don't ask me which one. I thought we had already replaced every part on that bus. It's been nothing but a pain the whole trip."

"Do you think it will make it to California?"

"I'm not sure it will ever move again, but I've thought that before. Pete keeps finding a way to get it to run … for a little while. I won't keep you from your pizza and spaghetti. I just wanted to say I was sorry for the disruption."

"Apology accepted," Adele said.

Lauren returned to her table, as Hope turned to the girls. "Let this be a lesson in manners. She didn't have to apologize, but she did. That shows some decent parenting."

"She doesn't belong with them," Lottie said.

"Why not?" Adele asked.

"Because she's too nice."

By the time Hope reached home, she had worked out what she wanted to say to Cori. "You know Max won't stay with us forever, right?"

Cori frowned. "He isn't leaving soon, is he?"

"Not yet. He'd like to stay a while longer, but one day, he's going to want to see his wife and daughter again, and then he'll leave."

Cori took a seat at the kitchen table. "It would be hard to have him leave. I'd miss him. We have good talks. He tells me about the past, and I tell him what it's like to be a teenager in today's world. A lot of people don't believe in ghosts. I feel lucky that we have one living in the house with us. It's sort of comforting."

"Some people believe in them ... sort of. History is filled with ghosts. I mean, the ancient Greeks and Romans believed in ghosts. Come to think of it, I'm not sure there were any cultures that didn't believe in spirits. I never believed in them until we moved here."

"I think it's pretty cool to have a ghost-friend." Cori stood. "Oh, I left my laptop in your office."

"I'll go up with you. I have some emails to send and lesson plans to check."

They went upstairs and entered the office, which was empty.

Hope said, "In the beginning when we first moved here, I thought I was going bonkers. When you first run into a ghost, you never believe your own eyes and ears. We've all been trained to not believe. So, we say we've had too much to drink, or we're on the wrong meds, or it was a trick of light and shadow. In the half-dark, you can see anything."

"I know what you mean about being surprised that ghosts are real. Most people wouldn't believe it."

"Since you're getting older and are starting to interact with more people, I want you to remember there are some rules."

"I thought so."

"What's the first rule about our ghost?" Hope asked.

"First rule is, I can't tell anyone about Max."

"Not for any reason. It has to be our secret. You can imagine what people would think and say, if we claim to know a ghost."

"Right, Mom. I've never told anyone about him, and I never will."

Hope held up two fingers. "Second, you can't hint about knowing that someone was killed here in this house."

"I remember."

Hope told her, "If people find out that you talk to

ghosts, they're going to put you in some sort of home or something. They'll think you're crazy. They won't want to interact with you. Third, don't tell Lottie. You may not tell her about him or let her see Max, not that he would let you."

"I know all this. I won't forget. Why are you bringing this up again?"

"Because you're getting older, and you might think you can impress someone by telling them there's a ghost in this house. You might be tempted to reveal his existence."

"I never would. I promise."

Max materialized standing at the window. "I never doubt that you will keep our secret."

Cori smiled and gestured at her mother. "But the worrywart sometimes worries."

"Exactly," Max said kindly. "That is because she's your mother."

10

Hope checked her emails and lesson plans while Cori and Max stayed in the attic office for over an hour talking together. Bijou rested on a blanket by the desk, but lifted her head whenever the two friends talked about something interesting. Cori always had a ton of questions about Max's life and he enjoyed telling her about things from his past.

"It would be kind of cool to bring my friends up here at Halloween and let you scare them to death." Cori chuckled at the thought.

Max said, "I understand, but I admit I take no pleasure in frightening people. I doubt you would enjoy it either, and your friends would never believe the truth. I'm afraid that you will find a great many ghosts are mean and nasty. I have heard that from other ghosts."

"I know," Cori said. "I was only kidding, but it would be cool to have kids see you on Halloween."

"Cori," Hope said, "someday, you might be tempted to brag about Max or claim you know ghosts are real. Don't give in. To protect everyone, you have to remain silent."

"I promise I'll never tell anyone."

"We trust you," Max added. "While staying here, I will do everything I can to make myself useful to you and your mother. I have become somewhat adept at researching the Internet. I can provide that sort of service to you, should you need it."

"She has to do her own research," Hope explained.

"Wait," Cori said, "Mom told me that you now know who killed you? You're satisfied that you have the right killers?"

Max nodded. "I have accepted the fact that your mother and I were correct when we learned about Davis Ellison and Margaret Ellison. They are the ones responsible for my early death."

"Bummer. But I'm glad you found out the truth and don't have to bother with that anymore."

Hope checked the time. "It's bedtime. You two

can continue your conversation tomorrow. I'll be down in a few minutes," she told her daughter.

"Good night, Max." Cori left the office with Bijou following after her.

After finishing her work in the office, Hope stopped by Cori's room where her daughter was already under the covers.

"I hope Max doesn't leave soon," Cori said.

Hope sat down on the bed. "I don't think he will. I asked him to stay. Since we moved here, he's become a friend and a bodyguard of sorts. He kept the house from burning down, and, while you can argue he did that to save himself, he also did it to save us. He likes you every bit as much as he likes me. That's the truth." Hope paused. "He will move on someday. He has to. It's how things work. I like to think all of us will know when that day has arrived. It will be one of those sad-happy days. Sad that he's leaving, happy that he's going on."

"Like when I go off to college?"

"Yeah, like that. Some things don't stay the same. It's the way it's supposed to be." A pang of sadness pulsed through Hope's heart.

∽

The next morning Hope was at the bakery working her special cake magic. Cori decided she'd rather stay at home with Max then go into the bakery with her mother. Hope was always impressed with how younger people accepted the impossible ... like the presence of ghosts ... far more readily than adults would. When her work was done and she returned to the house, she found Max and Cori playing a game of chess in the kitchen with Bijou sitting on a chair watching them.

"How's the game going?" Hope asked.

"Max is winning," Cori answered. "He's better than I am."

"Not for long," Max said. "Cori is catching onto my favorite moves."

The teen shook her head. "He's kidding you. He has me baffled most of the time."

Max glanced up from the game and paused to look at Hope and Cori. "You know, you two are the only family I have left. It seems everyone else has already moved on."

"We think the same about you, Max. We're glad you're here with us," Hope told him as she poured herself a cup of coffee.

When the two players returned to the chess

game, Hope asked her daughter, "Cori, have you finished your weekly chores?"

Cori rolled her eyes. "I'm playing chess with a ghost and you're asking me about chores?"

"They're not going to do themselves. Besides, you can play chess with Max any time … well, almost any time."

Max cocked his head to the side. "Someone is coming to the door. It's Lottie."

"Saved by the bell," Cori said. "Can I answer the door?"

"Yes, you may," Hope said. "But, you can't leave the house until the chores are finished. Maybe you can get Lottie to help you with them."

Cori snorted. "Doubt it. Lottie isn't big on chores." The teen dashed out of the room with the cat leading the way.

"I should go as well," Max said with a wink.

"I'll talk to you later," Hope said.

A minute later, Cori and Lottie entered the kitchen.

"Lottie," Hope said, "did you and your mom get your Christmas tree app fixed?"

Lottie looked at the chess board. "Have you started playing, Mrs. Herring?"

"I dabble," Hope answered.

"Cool. Mom talked to River this morning and he's going to check out the tag. He thinks it's broken or something. When he replaces it, he'll give us the new code."

"I'm surprised you didn't talk your mom into going out to visit your tree."

"I wanted to, but she said it wasn't necessary. Of course, if the new tag is halfway across the farm, she's going to make some calls."

"I'm sure it will be exactly where the old one was. I suppose Cori told you that she can't leave the house until she finishes her chores."

Lottie shook her head, and Cori frowned. Hope laughed. "You two figure it out."

Hope retreated to her office and her computer since she had some school tasks to complete. Max appeared as soon as she sat down.

"Lottie is staying for a bit?" Max patted Bijou.

"She is, so we'll keep our voices down. I don't want her finding out about you. I'm glad you and Cori have such a nice relationship. You mean a lot to her."

"The young do believe more readily, don't they?" Max looked pleased. "You do realize that you and Cori make my leaving that much more difficult."

"I do, and I'm glad for it. Although, I know you

won't hang around forever."

"I'm afraid I will become a frightful nuisance should I stay on too much longer. I have already sensed a loss of my faculties. I suppose that once the mystery was solved, I no longer needed to keep my mind sharp."

Hope reassured the ghost. "You have lost nothing. We all wonder sometimes if we are slowing down, both physically and mentally. In your case, I would guess that you have actually improved since you started surfing the net. Your brain is actually better."

"I'm glad you think so. I do enjoy you and Cori very much. For now, I shall leave you to your work."

Turning to her computer, Hope thought about how Max was a bit torn about staying. She promised herself she would not try to influence him ... at least, not too much.

An hour later, Cori appeared. "Hey, Mom, chores are finished. Lottie's mom wants to know if you can come over for a glass of wine before dinner."

"Dinner? Oh, right, we're invited for dinner. I forgot."

"We're going, aren't we?" Cori questioned.

"Of course. Sure, we'll go. I suppose you and Lottie are out the door, leaving me to follow along?"

"You don't really want to listen to us chat, do you? I mean, we're hardly as fascinating as what you're used to."

Hope knew Cori was referring to Max which made her smile. "How true. Tell Mrs. Wells, I'll be along in a few minutes."

"Roger that."

Shaking her head, Hope finished her work. She didn't shut down the computer, as Max would fill her seat as soon as she left.

"I'm going, Max. The Internet beckons you."

Max appeared. "Sometimes, I feel like a fish, Mrs. Herring. The net dangles some little tidbit, and I bite."

"It's called click bait. The headline or pic appeals to you, and you click the mouse. Some very clever people are behind the bait. Of course, the good thing is that even if you bite, you won't necessarily get landed. I suspect people click back to where they were all the time."

"It's truly addicting, isn't it?"

"Truly."

Max sat down at the desk, and Bijou remained in the attic with the man.

∾

Adele poured the red wine freely and Hope didn't stop her since it was Saturday night. She had an entire day to get sober.

"Do you watch Netflix?" Adele asked.

"Not much," Hope answered. "I'm afraid that if I get into that, I'll be binge watching every weekend."

"Exactly. They make such good movies and series. You get hooked, and two glasses of wine later, you're on episode five or something. I was watching a British series, and if it weren't for close caption, I wouldn't understand a word of dialogue. I thought we and the Brits both spoke the same language." Adele laughed.

"Cori tunes in sometimes, but I told her to be careful about what she watches."

"We raise them to do their own thinking, but young minds are mush. They are easily impressed and brainwashed."

Hope raised her glass to her lips. "I think our parents thought the same about us, and we've done all right."

"Speak for yourself, Hope. You manage to think a lot better than me. That's why you're so good at solving mysteries."

"I'm not so good. I just get lucky."

"Hah. Don't be so modest. Any time there's a

complicated murder around here, they call you. There's a reason for that."

Hope sipped from her glass and smiled. "I'm not so smart that I can figure out the Netflix mysteries."

Adele chuckled. "No one can." Her phone chimed, and she glanced at the ID. "It's River." She answered the call. "Yes, River, what's the verdict?"

Hope waited while Adele listened and jotted down a message. She read the number code back into the phone and nodded.

"Great, great," Adele said. "Thank you." She killed the connection and turned to Hope. "That was River at the tree farm. He gave me the code to the new tag he's putting on the tree. It should be online in the morning."

"Great. That will give Lottie something to do."

"Knowing Lottie, she'll text River as soon as she spots the new tag. Not necessary, but a way to keep her on River's radar."

"They have begun to think that way, haven't they?"

"I keep asking myself if my life with Lottie will hold up for one more week." Adele leaned back against the comfortable sofa.

"You mean, one more day," Hope said.

They both laughed.

11

It was Monday before Hope found out that Lauren was missing. She received a call from Detective Derrick Robinson, who gave her a few facts and asked if she would help.

"How exactly can I help?" Hope asked. "I mean, she's an adult and she's been missing how long, one day?"

"She's been missing about thirty-six hours. I know that doesn't sound like a long time, but she left because there was a fight. And, she left without any of her stuff, including her phone. What young person these days goes out without a phone?"

"Did anyone see where she was headed?"

"Out into the tree farm which abuts the conservation area with hundreds of acres of land. That means she might be lost or injured. The sheriff is forming a search party. We don't have to worry about that, but, he knows about you. He's already asked if you might be available, if there's some crime involved."

Hope heard something in Derrick's voice. "What aren't you telling me?"

"You are aware that Lauren was with the group currently staying at the farm?"

"Yes, I saw them arrive, and I witnessed a fracas at a restaurant. They weren't getting along."

"Precisely. It seems another person from the group has run off."

"Let me guess ... Conair."

"I believe that's what they call him, yes. Yesterday, he said he was going to look for Lauren. He left and didn't come back. The sheriff has alerted the law enforcement departments. Without a vehicle, we don't think Conair will get far."

"I'm guessing Lauren will show up today or tomorrow. She probably hitchhiked someplace and will realize that she needs her stuff," Hope suggested.

"I hope so. This is just a heads up. We simply don't have any evidence that it's anything more than a tiff that led to her stomping out."

"If you find out anything, keep me in the loop," Hope told the detective. "I'm not good at finding missing people, but I can try."

"You're good at everything. I'll be in touch."

On the way home from school, Hope told Cori about Lauren's disappearance.

"I think something bad happened to her," Cori said.

"That's premature. They have no evidence that anything happened."

"She went out all alone and never came back? Something happened to her, Mom. Someone in the woods spotted her, kidnapped her, and took her back to his dilapidated cabin, where he's going to make her his slave."

"You've watched too many TV shows. That doesn't happen very often in real life."

"She's gorgeous, Mom. Everyone can see that. If she's not in a cabin, then she's in some semi traveling across the country. The driver is just waiting for a chance to drive out into some desert and bury her body."

Hope's eyes widened. "I need to remind myself to review your viewing habits. Do you not watch the Christmas movies anymore?"

"No one watches the Christmas movies except

old people who have nothing else to do. Maybe, Lauren's hiding in the woods on purpose. Then, she can emerge at night and murder the other people from the magic bus."

"My, my, my, what's next? Lauren turns out to be an alien from some distant planet sent here to wreak havoc on the American Christmas tree farm?"

Cori crossed her arms over her chest. "Make fun all you want, but I'm telling you something bad happened to her."

"It's not a holiday season, Cori. What would Lauren's murder do to your favorite curse?"

"Let me think a minute. I'm sure there's some holiday somewhere that will fulfill the needs of the curse."

Hope said, "Candle Day in Tibet will not work. It has to be an American holiday, and you know it."

"Why is that?"

"Because I would venture that there's a holiday somewhere every day of the year. Even in this country, Congress is always designating a day as something-or-other day."

"You have a point. I just need to revise the curse. What if the curse applies because she disappeared on a Christmas tree farm? That's holiday related." Cori looked pleased with herself.

"True, but Christmas is three months away. You can't very well have a Christmas murder before Halloween or Thanksgiving."

"I'll have to think for a while longer. I'm sure there's a way the curse applies to this situation."

"Unless nothing bad has happened. Did you consider that? Perhaps, Lauren just needed to cool off. She may be back at the bus even as we speak."

"Not a chance," Cori said. "You need to listen to more true crime podcasts, Mom. If you did, you would know that bad things happen all the time, especially to pretty women. That's the real key. They're always pretty. Well, the young ones are."

"True crime? Don't we live that often enough?"

"Serial killers. They're everywhere."

Hope said, "It just seems like that because we know about them."

"You're wrong there. We don't know about the best serial killers, because they don't get caught. They're too smart."

"That's conjecture. Have you ever researched how many unsolved murders occur in a year?"

Cori shook her head. "Well, no, why would I do that? I'm scared enough the way it is."

"You might be less scared if you knew how many

killers might exist out of over three hundred million people living here."

"I never thought of it that way."

"Always good to know the facts. You can't judge your risk until you know the numbers."

Max and Bijou were in the kitchen when Hope and Cori arrived home.

"Hey, Max." Cori bent down to pat the cat. "How was your day?"

"Satisfactory, very satisfactory."

"Oh? What did you manage to do?"

"Nothing of real consequence, but I did watch a rather interesting video about the rabbit fence in Australia."

"Rabbit fence?"

"Yes, rabbits are not indigenous to Australia. They were imported in the nineteenth century. Australia was perfect rabbit country, so when some farmer released a few, they spread like wildfire. They couldn't be controlled, so the Aussies erected a fence to keep them out of certain areas. The fence is still there and quite long. I doubt it will keep the rabbits at bay for long."

"Wow, sort of like the Great Wall of China," Cori said.

"Yes, but just wire. Fences sound good, but they are not always effective."

"Very enlightening, Max," Hope said.

"The Internet is filled with amazing facts," Max said. "There is so much to learn. For now, I will leave you two to your work."

"Hey, Max," Cori said. "What about Dingos? Those are in Australia too, right?"

"I shall see what I can dig up on Dingos."

Max disappeared, leaving Hope and Cori in the kitchen.

"You know," Cori said, "I think I might be able to help Max with his learning."

"Oh, how might you do that?"

"I can feed him a few interesting topics to research. You know, feed his imagination."

Hope eyed her daughter. "These topics don't happen to be items you're going to write essays about, are they?"

Cori tapped her chin with her index finger. "Oh, I suppose there might be some overlap. That's almost impossible to avoid. You know, six degrees of separation or something."

"Make them ten degrees of separation, so Max doesn't become your personal research assistant."

"I would never even think of doing that."

Hope gave her daughter the side-eye. "Of course not, so you won't be disappointed when he doesn't come up with factoids you can use."

Cori frowned. "I wouldn't want to stifle his thirst for knowledge."

"Then, you won't curtail his serendipity either. Allow him to surf the Internet at will, understood?"

"Yes, Mom. Not doing my own research would be cheating, and, I never cheat."

"Well said, so make it well done."

Cori marched off to her room which prompted Hope to join Max in the attic.

"I just had a little discussion with Cori," Hope said. "She wants to use you to research the web for information she can use in school. I'm asking you not to indulge her. She has promised not to ask, but children often find ways around things. So, if she comes to you with some idea that might be fun to look up, make sure it's not something that will help her in school. Can I ask you to do that?"

"Why, of course, Mrs. Herring. I shall not acquiesce to Cori's requests. I understand the value of doing one's own work. Tom Sawyer might have enlisted the aid of others, but Cori won't have mine."

"Fair enough. If you can spare me a few minutes, I need to answer some email."

"Oh, yes, certainly. I apologize. I have become accustomed to using your computer exclusively. I must become more insightful."

"It's nothing, Max. In fact, it's probably time to get you your own computer. How does that sound?"

"I can hardly pay for a computer. And, of course, all the time I spend online must be reimbursed also."

"The Internet connection costs the same for three people as it does for one. So, never worry about that. As far as computers are concerned, Cori is always asking for an upgrade. So, what if we do this? I'll buy Cori a new computer, and you can use her old one."

"I may be mistaken, but that still costs you the price of a new computer."

"True, but I was going to buy it anyway. You're not costing me any more than I was already committed to. Although, I must warn you. Cori's computer is not state of the art. And, I don't know how long it will last. Computers are machines. They wear out and die. I'm just warning you."

"Mrs. Herring, I shall be most grateful for your efforts. Cori's computer will do nicely. I'm certain of that. My needs are small." He smiled. "I must confess that when you moved here, I had no idea we would become such friends. I had not had much success with other owners of the house. You have provided a companionship I had lost. I am forever in your debt."

"You might not be so grateful if Cori starts bossing you around." Hope smiled.

"That will not become a problem, Mrs. Herring."

Max disappeared, and Hope settled behind her computer. Not only did she have some email to process, but she needed to do some online computer shopping. She decided to enlist Cori in that effort. Cori would love to shop for a new laptop. All Hope had to do was set a price limit.

Smiling, Hope pulled up the first email. Why was it always the parent that asked about extra credit? Shouldn't the student pursue that? Some parents needed to back away and let their children speak for themselves.

Hope broached the computer topic as she and Cori prepared a dinner of salmon and broccoli. "I have a project for you," she began.

"Don't I have enough projects already?"

"I think you'll like this one. I'm certain you'll find time in your busy schedule for it."

"Mom, I'm overloaded the way it is. I mean, there are only so many hours in a day. Now, if you allowed me to stay home, say, two mornings a week, I'm sure I could accomplish everything you ask."

"If you're that busy, I suppose we'll just have to cut off visits to Lottie and watching TV. That should free up some hours."

"Since you put it that way, I agree that I have time for one more teeny-tiny project." Cori smiled. "I love to accommodate."

"Yes, well, your task is to find yourself a new computer."

Cori spun around to face her mother. "You're joking."

"Nope. Your current machine is aging, and, to be honest, Max needs his own computer. We share mine at the moment."

"A new computer? Cool. How much can I spend?"

Hope laughed. "Ah, yes, the inevitable constraint ... money."

"I don't need a desktop. A laptop will work great. That way, I can take it to the library and stuff."

"I agree. So, shop around. Don't look at the most expensive or the cheapest. Look for a middle-priced machine that will do what you need. I think you can figure that out. If not, go online and search according to use. There are lots of articles that can help."

"I'll do that. And, you're right, of course, I can find time to pick out a new laptop. Thanks, Mom."

"See, I knew it was simply a matter of motivation and priorities."

The doorbell rang.

"I'll get it." Cori ran out of the kitchen with Bijou galloping after her.

Hope called after her daughter. "If it's a salesman, tell him to go away."

Hope continued making dinner, rather pleased with herself. She had managed to make both Max and Cori happy. That was a good thing.

"It's not a salesman," Cori said as she entered the kitchen.

"I come for you."

Hope turned to the husky voice.

Across the room, Conair stood behind Cori, one hand on her shoulder. His other hand held a knife.

12

"What are you doing here?" Hope's heart was racing. "Put down that knife."

"You got to help me," Conair replied.

"No one can help you as long as you're holding my daughter at knifepoint. If you want anything at all, you have to let her go." Hope tried not to panic.

"I let her go, and you don't do anything for me. I'm no idiot. I've been around the cops before. I ain't gonna hurt her ... not if I don't have to."

"You're being stupid, Conair. That's your name, right? You know you're already in trouble. Don't make things worse."

"Listen to me." Conair waved the knife. "Listen to me. I got to tell you that I had nothin' to do with Lauren's going. That wasn't on me."

"I don't care." Hope's voice was firm. "We can't talk as long as you're threatening my daughter."

"You got to listen to me! The police talk to you."

"No one will talk to me or you, unless you drop that knife."

As Conair looked around the room, Hope spotted the desperation in his eyes. He was cornered, and he wasn't smart enough to figure his way out.

Bijou ran into the kitchen, arched her back, and hissed at the man.

"Look at me," Hope said. "Look at me. Let's stay calm and figure out how we're going to get what we want. You want to tell me your story, and, believe me, I want to hear it. But, you're holding my daughter. I don't hear so well when she's in danger. That's simple parenting. I'll tell you what. You let her go, just let her sit at the table, and I'll listen. I promise."

Conair frowned before he sat Cori in a chair. He didn't put down the knife, but it was no longer close to her throat.

"You better not be messin' with me," he said. "I don't like being messed with."

"No one is messing with you." Hope moved close to the stove where there was a skillet she hadn't yet used. "Now, start at the beginning. What are you to Lauren?"

"I ain't nothin'. That's just it. She's pretty and all, but she never paid no mind to me. I'm not stupid. I know when a gal is lookin' down on me."

"What did you fight about?"

"Drugs, booze, the usual."

Hope drummed her fingers close to the skillet handle. "Was she stealing from you? Was that it?"

"No, no, you got it all wrong."

"Ruffian!"

Conair turned to the voice and found Max standing a few feet away. Surprise filled Conair's face.

"What the…?"

That was all the distraction Hope needed. She grabbed the skillet and swung it hard against Conair's head.

But not hard enough.

Conair staggered, but he did not go down. Blood ran down his cheek, as he turned to Hope. He raised the knife and stepped toward her.

He didn't make it.

When Cori stuck out her foot, Conair tripped and fell to the floor, and Bijou jumped on the man and repeatedly bit him. That gave Hope time enough for a second blow with the skillet, and that did the trick. Conair was laid out on the floor, bleeding.

Hope wrapped her arms around her daughter and pulled her close. "Are you okay?"

"I'm fine, Mom."

They stood hugging one another for a few moments, then Hope said, "We need the duct tape to bind him."

"I'll get it." When Cori ran to the storage room, Hope kicked the knife from Conair's hand and looked at Max.

"Thank you for your help," she said to the ghost.

"I would have acted sooner, but he was too close to Cori."

"You did just fine, Max, just fine. Hang around for a minute or two, while we get this guy tied down."

"I trust you will not need to mention me to the police."

"No, no, Conair uses alcohol and drugs. I imagine he's had hallucinations before." Hope smiled at the ghost.

"Precisely what I was going to suggest," Max agreed.

Cori returned with the duct tape, and with her

help, Hope managed to tape Conair's wrists and ankles.

"Call 9-1-1," Hope told Cori. "I whacked him pretty hard."

"He deserved it," Cori said and turned to Max. "That was cool, Max."

Max beamed. "Thank you very much. And, now, I must go."

Max disappeared while Cori made the call. Hope grabbed an old towel and placed it under Conair's head. She had no desire to have him bleed all over her floor.

"They're coming," Cori said. "They'll be here soon."

"Before they get here, it was just you and me, right? Max wasn't here."

"Yes, and you swing a mean pan."

"Skillet, it's a skillet."

"Whatever. You were great. Wham, and down he went."

"You know what I mean. It's just us in here. No one else is in the house with us."

"Yeah, Mom, I know. It's not like the house is haunted or something." Cori winked.

"No jokes either."

Hope sat, her hands shaking, even as Conair moaned.

"Don't try to move," Hope told him. "The police and an ambulance are on the way. They'll take care of you."

"You ... you didn't have to smack me," Conair rasped. "I wasn't gonna hurt no one."

"You threatened to hurt us."

"Yeah, well. You got ibuprofen or something?"

Hope said, "The ambulance will be here soon."

"Was that a frying pan?"

"Skillet," Cori corrected.

"Ibuprofen, please."

"How's your eyesight?" Hope asked.

"Fine. I think. Can you cut off this tape? I can't feel my fingers."

"Soon, Conair, the EMTs will be here soon."

Conair moaned. "Who was that guy?"

"Who? Who do you mean?"

"The guy across the room. I didn't see him come in. Where did he come from?"

"There was no other person in the room," Hope said.

"But I seen him."

"You were hit on the head, hard. I suspect it scrambled your memory."

"I ... I guess maybe that's it. But, I seen him before I got whacked."

"Doesn't matter. Your memory was affected. Tell me about Lauren, while you have the chance."

"I might think better if I could feel my fingers."

"When they take you, you won't have another chance to tell me anything," Hope warned.

"Yeah, yeah, I guess that's true." Conair closed his eyes, as if trying to remember. "Lauren and me been fighting since she got on the bus. Me and Sky tried to tell Pete that Lauren was gonna be trouble. A woman like that stirs up things. They're no good on the road."

"Pete wanted her on the bus?"

"Heck, yeah. You seen her. What man is gonna kick her off?"

"So, the three of you fought over Lauren?"

"We had words. I tried to steer clear, but she didn't like that. She'd flirt and stuff, and I would think she liked me. Then, she would laugh in my face. She laughed in all our faces. She fooled everyone with her smile. Led us on like dogs until she got tired of playing. No one really liked her."

"No one liked her unless she was being nice?" Hope asked.

"Yeah, that's about right. I got so I ran whenever

she tried to move close. You get burned often enough, then you run from matches. That's what we was jawin' about in the restaurant. We wanted to get shut of her."

"She didn't want to leave?"

"She got nowhere to go. Not that she needed a place. You saw her. She could get a tiger to give up his stripes. She didn't need nothin'."

Hope couldn't tell where Conair's truth ended, and the lies started. He was like a dog that had been kicked too many times. He was always trying to protect his hide.

"So, everyone hated her. Enough to harm her?"

"Sky once told me she was gonna cut Lauren's face to ribbons. Sky hated Lauren. I saw once when Pete pulled a punch and hit a wall instead of that face. Lauren just laughed. It weren't just them. Pete's brother caught the fever, too. He fell all over himself trying to impress Lauren."

"That must have caused a problem in the house."

"Oh, yeah. His wife yelled at him all the time. She wanted the bus and Lauren as far away as they could get. You know how some wives are. She was jealous and scared. She asked me if I could make Lauren disappear. I told her I would rather wrestle the devil. She wanted that girl gone."

"So, basically, Lauren had no friends on the farm, right?"

"Wrong, we was all her friends. We just hated ourselves for doing what she wanted. People never said no to Lauren."

"You all wanted her gone?"

"Yeah, but none of us had the guts to get that done."

The doorbell rang, and Cori ran to answer it.

"That will be the police," Hope told Conair. "If I were you, I'd tell them everything you told me. That would be a good start."

"Yeah, maybe, but police and me don't get along."

Seconds later, a young man and a young woman in uniforms entered the kitchen. They took one look and frowned.

"He had a knife." Hope pointed. "It's over there. I hit him with a skillet."

"You can wait in another room if you want," the female officer said.

"Thank you." Hope passed the EMTs, as she headed for the family room where Cori was waiting.

"Did he kill her?" Cori asked.

"We don't know if Lauren is dead," Hope answered. "I doubt that she is. I'm pretty sure he didn't kill her, but he might know more about where she went."

"Why did he come here?"

"I think he was trying to get ahead of the law. He wanted to convince me he had nothing to do with Lauren's disappearance. Someone told him I solved murders here."

"You do."

"Sometimes."

"All the time."

Hope waited with Cori until Detective Robinson joined them. He looked a bit harried, but he smiled.

"You did a bang-up job with Conair," the detective said. "He came to threaten you why?"

"I'm guessing he thought I could help him convince you that he had nothing to do with Lauren's disappearance."

"With a knife?"

Hope shrugged. "He isn't the best thinker in the world."

"I suppose not. Did he tell you anything interesting?"

"Yes, he said that everyone at the farm had a love-hate relationship with Lauren."

"I can see where that could happen."

"They all wanted to get rid of her for various reasons."

"Nice folks to hang with. Tell me more."

Hope repeated what Conair had told her. Detective Robinson took notes and occasionally asked a question. Hope filled in the best she could.

"What do you think? Did Conair harm her?" the detective asked.

"I honestly don't know. He might have, and is clever enough to come to me to plead his case. He might reason that a guilty man would just run. Talking to me would bolster his innocence."

"He's not that smart ... I don't think."

"Neither do I, but it would explain why he brought a knife and not a gun."

"He never intended to do anything but threaten?"

"That would make sense."

The detective rubbed his face. "He's going to jail and will probably be charged with felony attempted murder. The lawyers will argue about that and get it reduced to some lesser crime. In the meantime, you're safe. If we find Lauren's body, he might be charged with murder, especially if she died from a knife wound."

"If he did kill her, I would think he'd be west of the Mississippi by now," Hope offered.

"Yes, that makes sense. I'll check into the others. Seems they all had a motive, and probably opportunity. I know I'm putting the cart before the horse, as we haven't found Lauren yet."

"Nothing wrong with questioning people about someone missing."

"It's just that they might be more cooperative if we had a body as leverage. Not that I'm wishing she were dead. Nothing like that at all."

The EMTs pushed a gurney past. Conair was strapped on top, head bandaged and wrists untaped. He glanced over and half smiled, which told Hope nothing.

"If you think of anything more," Detective Robinson said, "call me tomorrow."

"I'll make sure," Hope told him.

The house emptied of the emergency personnel, Hope locked the door, and met Cori in the kitchen.

"Hungry?" Hope asked.

Cori nodded. "I am now. That was kind of crazy, wasn't it?"

Hope pulled pot pies from the freezer. "These will have to do. And, yes, that was a little on the bonkers side."

The Christmas Tree Farm

"I don't think he killed her."

"Why not?"

"I'll say it this way. I don't think he has the courage to kill her. He does drugs, and he might kill animals and stuff. He might even harm someone under the right circumstances. But I don't see him as a killer."

"You're probably right," Hope said. "But, if it was some kind of accident, he might well finish her off and hide the body."

"I didn't think of that. You mean, like they were arguing or something? Like Conair got upset and hit her without thinking?"

"People do stupid things when they're angry."

"Don't I know it. At school, one of the boys actually got into a fight with Mr. Harvey, the gym teacher. That wasn't smart at all."

Max appeared in the corner of the room. "Didn't that work out just dandy? We are a good team." He grinned.

13

"Thank you for helping us, Max," Cori said.

"No, thank your mother. She sent me a clear signal. I did nothing but distract a man who could not harm me in any way. It was your mother that proved decisive."

"I wouldn't have had the chance without you, Max," Hope told him.

"Then, as I said, it was a team effort." Max nodded.

"I didn't do anything," Cori said. "Except, get captured by the big lug."

"Brilliant ploy," Max said. "Completely kept the hooligan off balance. Using the duct tape was appropriate also. The thug needed to be incapacitated. I commend you, Mrs. Herring, on insisting that the skillet had, indeed, altered the man's memory. That ended what might have been uncomfortable questions from the constable."

"Detective, but no matter. He was never going to believe Conair. No one will. That's the problem with being an untamed liar. No one believes you."

"I will not keep you," Max said. "I simply wanted to bask in a bit of glory for a minute or two. I had forgotten just how satisfying it can be to give someone the comeuppance they deserve."

Max disappeared, and Hope turned to Cori.

"I think I like Max even more than before." Cori smiled.

"Let this be a lesson. Max will be here to help, but you must not call upon him unless the situation is dire. We don't want to expose him."

"Don't worry, Mom. I'll keep him safe."

Later that night when Hope was in bed, she considered what Conair had revealed. It seemed everyone associated with Lauren hated her. Conair made her into a wormy apple—gorgeous on the outside, rotten on the inside. She was a femme fatale who used her beauty as a weapon. Hope knew of such women, although she had never befriended one. Who could befriend a woman like that?

Yet, somehow, Conair's description didn't ring

true. It seemed more sour grapes than accurate observation. Not that it made much difference. Hope was almost convinced that Lauren had simply walked away from people who no longer interested her. Perhaps, they really didn't like her. Conair certainly didn't. How long would it be before she showed up somewhere else?

Hopefully soon. Hope didn't want either the people at the farm or the authorities to be wallowing in doubt.

The next morning, she fielded a call from Detective Robinson before classes began. He informed her that Conair was stable and going to be just fine, even if he would suffer from headaches for a few days. Conair also claimed he had no idea what had happened to Lauren. He guessed she had run off, because the others were being mean to her. That was hokum, but Conair stood by it. The detective also said that they would be searching the farm later, looking for any clues, but he wasn't overly optimistic. Hope appreciated the call, but she had never worried about Conair being a problem in the future.

The second call from Detective Robinson arrived as Hope was leaving for the day.

"We found a shirt," the detective said. "We believe Lauren was wearing the shirt when she disappeared. That has not been verified, although she did own one like it."

"Did the shirt say—'Goodbye, Did You Say Something?'"

"Yes, it does. How did you know?"

"She was wearing it in the restaurant the other night."

"Well, this one is like it. The only difference being that this one has blood stains on it."

"Her blood?" Hope asked.

"We don't yet know."

"Where was it found?"

"On the west end of the farm, next to a state highway."

"But, no body?" Hope questioned.

"No, just the shirt. Any ideas?"

"Well, the highway adds something, doesn't it?"

"Yes, I was thinking that maybe she tried to hitchhike or something and ran into some trouble. Although, she didn't need to hitchhike. If she was just walking, someone might have stopped."

"That sounds about right," Hope agreed. "Someone wanted to pick her up, and she fought, and well, lost her shirt in the process."

"Or someone dumped her in a car or van or something and took off. Might have been several people involved. You know, a snatch and grab kidnapping," the detective said.

"Walking on the wrong road at the wrong time."

"But, why would they leave the shirt? That doesn't make much sense, does it?" Derrick asked.

"They might leave it if they were just trying to plant some sort of false clue," Hope offered.

"We need to know if it's her blood."

"Was the shirt hidden?" Hope asked the detective.

"Hidden? No, not really, just sort of thrown under a tree."

"What if she cut herself somehow? She bled all over her shirt, so she dumped it under a tree. She went to the highway and flagged down someone. Who's going to drive away from a pretty woman in a bra? They'd pick her up and drive her somewhere," Hope guessed

"To the hospital."

"Yep, that would make sense to me."

"We checked the hospital. No one matching her description was treated."

"So, she didn't make it to the hospital. The Good Samaritan took her to their house for treatment? Make sense?" Hope wondered aloud.

"It does, but our Good Samaritan didn't call the sheriff or anyone else for that matter."

Hope thought aloud. "Perhaps, she wasn't able to tell them who she was. She might have fainted or lost blood or, well, anything."

The detective said, "I would think most people would still call the cops."

"You're right. Most people would. I don't know. I can't figure it out. We don't know enough. Have you checked with every hospital in the county? The surrounding counties?"

"Not yet, but I'll have it done. Urgent care facilities, too. If the bleeding wasn't too bad, she might have ended up there."

"Detective, I'm supposing that she's injured, but still alive."

"So am I, Hope. I don't want to go full murder code yet. For all we know, she ditched one shirt and found another somewhere. I don't think there was a fatal amount of blood on the shirt."

"That's encouraging. You can query all the medical facilities around. You might just find her. Like Conair, she might have simply banged her head, bled all over her shirt, and found her way to some sort of help."

"Or, she wandered off the farm and into the

woods. If she had a concussion, she might have blacked out. We'll expand the search tomorrow. Perhaps, the dogs will pick up her scent."

"I hope so. I hate to think of her lying under some tree, bleeding from a head wound. There are critters out there."

"We're all well aware of that."

Hope said goodbye to the detective, picked up Cori at her school, and headed home.

"I don't think she's in the woods." Cori watched out the window as the SUV moved down the road.

"Why not?"

"Because, the road is close by. I can see her stumbling down the berm or something but not into the woods."

"That would make sense, if she was aware enough to tell the difference."

"Can I go to Lottie's when we get home?" Cori asked.

"Homework finished?"

"Almost."

"Then, you're almost at Lottie's. Just a few more minutes, and it will be done."

"You're no fun."

"Mothers weren't designed to be fun. Mothers

who try to be fun generally don't do well with their children."

"You really think so?"

"I do. When you have children, I hope you think so, too. Your kids will have friends. They need parents."

"I don't know if I'll have kids."

"Oh, why not?"

"Climate change."

"Climate change?"

"Humans are polluting everything and making the planet heat up, and pretty soon all the animals will die off. We'll have nothing but ashes and misery. I don't know if I can contribute to that. We're told the heating is unprecedented."

Hope said, "There have been several climate incidents over the ages."

"Such as?"

"The Little Ice Age, the Roman heat wave, the medieval heat wave, the Ice Age itself. What I want you to realize is that most people have no concept of the past, of history. They grow up and think the world has always been this way. We live in a very rare, very small snippet of time, a snippet of luxury."

"Luxury?" Cori questioned.

"It doesn't seem like that sometimes, I know, but

we live in unparalleled luxury. Just a few hundred years ago, people didn't eat three meals a day. They didn't have indoor plumbing."

"Yuck."

"No radio, phone, TV, central heating or air, not even screens on the windows—mostly no glass windows. Disease, pain, misery, no artificial joints or limbs, primitive medicine at its best. Just a few hundred years ago."

"Your point?"

"Don't assume that the world has always been the way it is now. It hasn't been. To be clear, it won't stay this way. It might get better, it might get worse, but it won't be the same."

"Humans are changing the planet."

"I know that. But did you also know that there are more trees in the United States now than there were in nineteen hundred?"

"True?"

"True. People burned wood for heat and cooking, so they felled trees. When they switched to coal, oil, and gas, they no longer cut down the trees. When people moved from paper to other forms of communication, millions of trees were saved. It's not hard to understand. Simple, really. People didn't cut down trees for fun. It was need."

"You don't think we're killing the planet with plastic and fossil fuels?" Cori asked.

"Yes, I do, but go back a hundred years. The air was dirtier. The water was more contaminated. We don't have soot and ash raining down on us. We don't have garbage and sewage filling the gutters of our streets. Well, not most of our streets. By many measures, the country is much cleaner now, healthier, too. I believe we'll get better at keeping the world cleaner. I think we'll figure it out. I really do."

"I hope you're right."

Hope said, "Me, too. You might talk to Max also. He lived before the invention of our modern conveniences. See what his views are. No one who was thirty or forty years old in 1920 is alive today—except Max."

"That's a great idea."

As Hope pulled into her driveway, she noticed the person sitting on the front porch, rocking back and forth in one of the white rockers.

"Who's that?" Cori asked.

"I believe the people on the bus called her Sky."

14

Hope handed Sky a beer and pulled another white rocker closer to the woman.

"Thank you," Sky said. "You have a very nice house here."

"Would you rather sit inside?"

"No, no, I like the outside better. When I was little, I was always out in the yard, playing with whatever toy I could make from the branches and sticks that fell from the trees. We lived in West Virginia, coal country. It was a hard scrabble farm that never amounted to spit, if you know what I mean. Pa worked with the coal. Mom worked on babies. When you live in a small cabin with a bunch of kids, you learn to appreciate the outdoors."

Sky sipped the beer and rocked. "I know you

don't want to listen to all this, but I want you to understand. I'm like the others, well, all but Lauren. I've been jailed, and it liked to kill me. You should know why."

"I'll listen."

"I left school when I was ten. It wasn't any sort of hardship. I missed half the days I was supposed to be there. Ma and Pa didn't put much store in books and learning, and I was happier running around on the mountain. I knew how to read and write. I figured I didn't need much more than that. Lots of kids on the mountain thought the same way. Lots of kids.

"I left the mountain when I was fourteen. Ma wanted to marry me off to some distant cousin on the next mountain over. I knew what being married was all about, and I didn't want a passel of kids pulling at my jeans. I hitched to Florida, because it was warm. I was pretty stupid back then. I got picked up by a dude with a nice mustache and a tent. That suited me fine. He wasn't much for work, so we stole from other folks. That didn't feel right, but Bo said 'good people would give us the stuff anyway. We're just saving them the carrying charge or whatever.' Bo could make pilfering candy bars from the 7-Eleven sound like doing a preacher's work. That led to my first run-in with the law. You get let free only so many times before they decide you haven't learned your lesson. That was the worst ninety days of my life. I wanted to die. I asked God to take me. He didn't."

Sky paused, and Hope didn't press for more. Some people couldn't tackle something directly. They had to circle a few times, before they made their point.

"I won't bore you with all the details. Let's just say that I got better at not getting caught, mainly because I left towns and states before the cops could catch me. No one is going to come after you for a petty theft charge. When I reached California, I thought I had found my paradise. An outdoor girl could be happy there. I joined a commune where I worked hard and lived hard and discovered I had a knack for gardening. That was fun. Communes don't last long. There is no making sure that everyone contributes equally. Can't happen. Then, you get arguments, and arguments lead to breakup. People move on. I moved on ... to the next commune. It was predictable and mostly fun.

"I once heard someone say that something moving along, keeps moving along. It's physics or something. I kept moving along. Made it from one coast to the other. Ended up in Maine, where I took up with Pete and Conair. Pete had a vision, and a bus. He said he was driving to California, and I was welcome to come with him. I'm not as young as I once was. I thought California would work good for me. I had never really lost my love for it. We headed south ... and picked up Lauren."

Sky finished her beer and held up the empty can. Hope took the empty and retrieved a full can from the kitchen. Sky hadn't moved or stopped rocking.

"I shouldn't say we picked up Lauren. More like she picked up us. We hadn't gone thirty miles before the bus needed a tire. She was working in a diner across the street. She walked over and asked where we were going. She still had on her waitress uniform. When Pete said California, she asked if she could come. You tell me how anyone says no to Lauren. We picked her up on the way out of town. She was as sweet as molasses on the outside. Inside, she was a mountain rattler. One state later, we was all yelling at each other. Some people are like that. Too clever for their own good."

Sky looked over, and Hope waited. The story wasn't over.

"That's not why I came to you. Pete's brother told all of us about how you solve murders and mysteries.

Conair said he was going to talk to you. I told him it was a bad idea, but he wouldn't listen."

"If you thought it was a bad idea, why are you here?" Hope asked.

"I guess you've heard how none of us got along too well with Lauren. I've seen that before. She didn't like to pull her weight, and, frankly, she could always get one of the guys to do it for her. No real harm in that, except it breeds discontent. Discontent is a disease that kills off friendships. Plain and simple. Happens every time."

"That still doesn't explain why you're talking to me."

"Lauren didn't run off."

"How do you know that?"

"You ever watch monkeys? I've been to a lot of zoos. I like zoos. I guess you might say I get along better with animals than I do humans. I'm not proud of that. It just is. Anyway, the monkeys are my favorite. They're always out, and they're always jumping around, bothering each other, eating and sleeping. Sometimes, they get along good, sometimes they don't, like people. Where monkeys aren't like people is when they jump. A monkey jumps only when there's another limb to jump to. They don't jump on faith. Lauren was like a monkey. She wasn't going to jump unless there was another bus pulling up to take her. Know what I mean?"

"I do. I'm guessing that Lauren could almost always find that next bus."

"Exactly. And, she wouldn't leave without her stuff. No need for that."

"If she didn't run off, where is she?"

"She's dead, as near as I can tell."

"Not hurt? Not hiding out?"

"Nope," Sky said. "And, since she's dead, someone she knew killed her."

"Not some trucker who spotted her from the road?"

"Lauren might charm some trucker to take her to Miami, but she wouldn't leave without her goods."

"Okay, let's say you're right. Why are you here?"

"Same reason Conair came. I want you to know about me, about why the cops will want to hold me in jail."

"Why?" Hope asked.

"When they go digging, they're gonna find Theodore Roosevelt."

"Teddy Roosevelt?"

"Yeah, he changed his name because he thought Teddy was the man Theodore wanted to be. Didn't come out that way, but not because Theodore didn't try. I won't bore you with details. We was driving across country in an old pickup that Theodore had cheated some old lady out of. Doesn't matter how he did it. He just did. We got to Arkansas, stopped some place for the night. Pitched a tent and unrolled the sleeping bags. There are a lot of stars at night, especially out in the middle of nowhere. Theodore liked to find God in the stars. He said the stars proved there was a higher presence. I never found God there, but then, I never looked too hard. When the sun rose, Theodore was gone. I didn't know where. I waited around, cause that's what you do. In the middle of the afternoon, the farmer who owned the land found me. He asked, I explained, and he called the cops."

Hope studied Sky, who looked out over the street, watching. Perhaps she was counting birds or imagining the figures clouds made. Hope was trying to figure out the woman.

"The cops questioned me, and I answered truthfully," Sky said. "They talked to the farmer for a while. We all agreed that I would stay with the truck for a day or two and wait for Theodore to return. I didn't like it, but it was better than being hauled to town. I knew right off that Theodore wasn't coming back. Well, I didn't know, but I felt like that. Two days later, they searched high and low for Theodore. No dice. He was gone. They grilled me for a while, but I was no help. I didn't even know his real name. In the end, they turned me loose, but they kept the truck. It belonged to Theodore."

Sky turned and looked Hope in the eye.

"I want you to know this because I've been involved in a disappearance before. I didn't do anything. I don't know if they ever found Theodore or his body. But, they're going to try and blame me. That's human nature. A rooster does what a rooster does. I didn't do anything to Theodore, and I didn't do anything to Lauren."

"What aren't you telling me?"

Sky half smiled. "I knew you would figure it out, but I had to try. No hard feelings?"

"Tell me."

Sky turned away. "When they test the blood on Lauren's shirt, they're going to find out that it's mine, some of it."

"Go on."

"We had words. I was drinking, and she was being Lauren. I told her she should leave and go off on her own. She didn't like that. She told me to be nice, or she would have Conair cut me. Conair was like her pet snake. She said she could make him do anything. That got me riled, so I punched her. Right on the nose. She started to bleed. We was in the bus, so she grabbed one of Pete's boots and whacked me across the face. That made me bleed. We wrestled for a bit, both of us bleeding, but that didn't come to anything. We grew tired and broke it off. She left the bus, and I drank more. I hit her sure, but I didn't kill her."

"She wasn't hurt?"

"Just her nose, and it's not like I broke it. People bleed out the nose all the time."

"True. You didn't follow her?"

"Not a chance. I got busy packing. I figured that Pete would kick me off the bus as soon as he found out."

"No one else was there?"

"Not that I saw." Sky stood. "I'll be going."

"Is any of what you told me true?"

Shy shrugged. "Some of it. Most of it. The part about Theodore is true. You have to believe that. I don't know what happened to him."

With that Sky walked off the porch, leaving Hope to wonder if the woman was going to walk right on out of Castle Park, maybe right out of North Carolina. Hope had no doubt that Sky's blood would be found on Lauren's shirt. The question was how it really got there. A cat fight in an old bus? Or a battle to the death somewhere else? Hope remembered the first rule of interrogation.

People lied.

They lied because the truth was inconvenient or hurtful, or maybe they just embellished an old memory.

Even under oath, people lied. Sometimes, they lied so much and so often that they came to believe the lie. It sounded so much better than the truth.

Hope found Max and Cori in the kitchen.

"I thought you were going to Lottie's," Hope said.

"I was," Cori answered. "Then, I started asking Max questions. He told me he grew up without any indoor plumbing."

"Cori finds that terribly primitive," Max said. "I have assured her that in the rural areas, it was quite common."

"I'm sure Max can tell you all about how the world was a hundred years ago. While he does, think about what you want for dinner. I have to make a call."

Hope went to her attic office before she dialed.

"Detective Robinson," Hope said. "Have you tested the blood on Lauren's shirt yet?"

15

"I don't yet have the final results, why do you ask?"

Hope replied, "Sky, the woman from the bus, talked to me a little while ago, and she said she had an altercation with Lauren. Both women bled, so Sky's blood is likely on the shirt. If you don't yet have a sample of her blood, you might want to get one."

"That's interesting. Anything else?"

Hope passed along the stories Sky had revealed, while the detective listened patiently until she'd finished.

"You believe her?" he asked.

"Yes and no. Yes, I think she had a tough life. Did she tell the absolute truth? I doubt it. People embellish and leave things out. The truth lies somewhere in between."

"You're right about that. I'll make sure to get a blood sample from Sky. If she offers more, so be it. I'm still not convinced anything bad happened to the woman."

"We can only do what we can do."

A few more words and they ended the call. Hope had the feeling she had performed just as Sky wanted ... she was supposed to share the information. It was an indirect confession of ... something, but Hope wasn't sure of what.

In the kitchen, Max was teaching Cori how to make his favorite stew, and the two stood at the counter chatting and laughing.

"That smells delicious," Hope told them.

"Your daughter is a natural," Max said.

"He's lying. He's doing all the hard work," Cori said. "But, it does smell good, doesn't it?"

"Traditional Brunswick Stew uses squirrel," Max explained. "We are not squirrel hunters, so we improvised with beef. This is close to the Three Sisters stew, aptly named for corn, beans, and squash, which are the main ingredients. Actually, the vegetables were always the heart of stews. Whatever game meat might be available was tossed in. Simmer for a while, and you have something that will keep you warm on a cold, winter night."

"Well, it's not winter yet," Hope said. "But, that doesn't mean we can't share a wonderful stew."

"Exactly."

"I need to do some homework," Cori said. "How long before the stew is ready?"

"I should think another half hour will do," Max said. "Half the fun of making stew is the savory aroma. It makes everyone hungry."

"I'll second that."

Cori left, and Max turned to Hope. "That woman who spoke to you? She is of the group that arrived by bus?"

"Yes, she traveled with the woman who's missing. I'm not sure what she wanted to accomplish by talking to me, but it hardly matters. She's not going anywhere in the near future."

"Do you think you'll find the missing woman alive?"

"The woman who came here doesn't think so. She claims that Lauren wasn't the type to just up and go. She was a monkey. She always knew where she was going to land."

"Hmm, like our squirrels. They jump from tree to tree, but they rarely miss. Some people are like that."

"And some miss almost every time. There is no

accounting for some things, Max. The daredevil versus the titmouse, which one will succeed? There's no good way to know."

"I agree. Have you given any thought to Cori's new computer?" Max questioned.

"Not yet. Why don't you and Cori figure that out? Search the net, find a machine that will suit her needs, and email me the specifics. If I can swing the cost, I will."

"Excellent idea. Half the fun of shopping is the search, if I'm not mistaken. Everyone likes to handle the merchandise before they jump."

Hope chuckled. "And discover they never wanted the item in the first place."

"I once thought of marriage that way," Max said. "In my day, you could do only so much shopping before you were expected to choose someone. Sometimes, I think this era does things correctly. Move in, test the waters, and if there is love and compatibility, then marriage should be the logical conclusion."

"Marriage is not so popular as it once was. I suppose that can be attributed to the fact that women have become more independent. They don't need a mate in order to live well."

"I can think of little worse than an unfulfilling marriage, Mrs. Herring. It is like a jail sentence with no chance of parole. It is a wonder that we don't have more murders than we have."

"What do you think of this idea? What if every couple were required to use some kind of aging app to portray themselves forty years into the future? Would a good likeness scare them off or entice them?"

"I know few people who became more handsome with age. I, for one, would think a future likeness would be very interesting. I mean, we change slowly, so slowly that we hardly notice. It's only when we see old photographs of ourselves that we fully understand the transformation, and, by then, it hardly matters. We have become what we were meant to become."

"Well said, Max. You're right."

"I will leave you to the stew," Max said. "It reminds me of … well, of…" He vanished before finishing his sentence.

While Hope set the table, she couldn't help but wonder about Lauren. What had happened to the young woman? Was she still alive? Had someone killed her? Only time would tell.

∿

On the drive to school the next day, Hope broached the topic of River Soames.

"How's River doing?" she asked.

"He's acting funny," Cori answered. "I mean, he's older, so I don't expect him to say much to me, but, he hasn't said much to anyone. He sits by himself at lunch. When people try to sit by him, he moves. It's weird."

"There's a lot going on at the tree farm with the police, and searchers, and everything. You can't blame him for wanting a little alone time. I'm guessing he's been questioned more than once."

"I know, and I don't press him or anything. I just think he might feel better if he opened up a little. Holding it in doesn't seem to be a very good strategy."

"Everyone has his or her own level of tolerance," Hope pointed out.

"What does that mean?"

"It means that we all have a pain threshold. What bothers one person might not bother the next. Some people hold in things, until they become too big to tolerate."

"Then, what happens?"

"Different things. Some people explode, some break down, some find another person to share things with, which would seem to be the best way to handle any sort of problem or upset."

"Why can't we all just be a little more simple? People make a big deal out of everything."

"Remember that the next time disappointment taps you on the shoulder."

"Sometimes, I think it sits on my shoulder like a parrot. Max told me about your idea. He and I are going to hunt down a new laptop after school."

"Great. Not too expensive, please."

"Don't worry, Mom, it won't come gilded with gold," Cori kidded.

Hope knew that one of the pluses of teaching was that when she was in the classroom, she didn't think about other things. The outside world was the outside world. It didn't encroach upon her lessons. Her students were not so thankful, as they often tried to visit the other world through phones and tablets. Hope wanted to tell them that there would come a time when they would curse their phones and leave them behind whenever possible. Being at the beck and call of a boss was not enticing.

After school, Hope found Detective Robinson standing on the sidewalk out front.

"Hope," the detective said, "I was in the neighborhood, and I wanted to let you know that we did

ID some of the blood as coming from Sky. A small portion of the blood. The bulk of the blood was most likely Lauren's. There were several other blood stains that we have yet to ID. When we do, I'll let you know."

"Is anyone at the farm not cooperating as far as blood is concerned?"

"I'm about to find out. The sheriff sent a deputy to collect samples from Pete Soames, his brother, and his sister-in-law. If they suddenly balk, that might tell us something."

"Did you consider that someone might have added some blood on purpose? After the shirt was taken off Lauren?"

"Taken?"

"Lauren is a beautiful woman, but I didn't get the vibe that she liked to walk around half naked. A bloody shirt would still be wearable. Someone might have taken it and purposefully added some blood in order to confound the forensic techs."

"Anything is possible. But, why would someone do that? I mean a killer might try that, but we don't know if she is indeed dead."

"Do you think Lauren did it herself? Did she want us to think something bad happened to her?"

"I've considered that. But, why? Why would she

deliberately muddy the water? I can think of only one reason. She wanted someone to be blamed and arrested."

Hope asked, "Revenge comes in all flavors and colors, doesn't it? Have you spent any time at the tree farm?"

"A little, why?"

"I wondered if there was an uptick in business. Do they have more customers coming out to the farm?"

Derrick raised an eyebrow. "Do you think this is some kind of stunt to get the farm name in the papers and on TV?"

"A beautiful woman disappears, leaving no note or even much of a clue. Just a bloody shirt. That has to generate some public interest."

"It's a stretch, isn't it?"

"In December 1926, Agatha Christie disappeared for eleven days. To this day, no one knows what happened to her. I think she claimed some form of amnesia. She never explained where she was or what was going on during the days she was missing."

"So, Lauren will walk out of the trees and say she can't remember where she's been? It was all done to gin up some Christmas tree sales?"

"History is full of stories about promoters who

dreamed up schemes to get free publicity. Would I be surprised? Not really. We're not talking about a group of people known for their truthfulness."

"You make a good point." Derrick sighed. "The farm has probably never been so busy. People are out there among the trees, hoping to stumble on a corpse."

"People are curious. Every car wreck has its gawkers. Every fire draws spectators. Frankly, if it is a stunt, that's pretty much all right with me. Sure, everyone is out some energy and time, but that's better than a murder."

"When that woman shows up, she better have one heck of a story. Otherwise, there are some charges that will be leveled."

The detective left, and Hope headed to her SUV. Did she really think Lauren's disappearance was some kind of bid to increase the number of Christmas tree buyers? According to Conair and Sky, Lauren wasn't the kind of person to offer help to anyone but herself. Who would pay Lauren to vanish for a few days? The answer to that was simple.

The Soames family.

Not Pete so much, but River and his parents would benefit. Hiring a beautiful woman to become a missing person might be a good investment. Who would know if Lauren was coached well enough to fake a lost memory? She was wandering around in the woods. Sooner or later, she would wander out of the woods. That was both good and bad ... but mostly good.

As soon as Hope and her daughter reached home, Cori ran up to the attic to confer with Max. They were both dedicated to finding the perfect laptop. Max had the advantage of being home all day. There were any number of articles that rated and ranked various computers. Armed with that information, along with the reviews buyers left online, would steer Max away from the lemons. Would it pinpoint the perfect machine? Hope didn't think so, but a laptop didn't need to be perfect.

That night, as Hope stared at the ceiling waiting for sleep, she considered her role in Lauren's disappearance. Did Hope have one? There was very little information to act on. A woman walked off into the woods and didn't come back. She remembered that Sherlock Holmes had once said that a crime with many details was easier to solve than one without telltale signs. Finding a corpse on the sidewalk at midnight might prove far more difficult to solve than the death of some official in his bed.

Facts.

Hope needed facts.

She wasn't sure they would help because something inside her head told her Lauren wouldn't be coming out of the woods.

16

After school the next day, Hope found Cori sitting on a low wall, talking to River Soames. She noticed the animation in her daughter's face as she and River smiled at one another.

"Hey, Mrs. Herring," River said as Hope approached. "Cori's been telling me about the holiday murder curse. Sounds freaky."

"Don't believe her, River. I think it's safe to say there's no such thing as a holiday murder curse."

"She makes it sound real though."

Cori spoke up. "I'm just pointing out the coincidences of murders that have occurred right around a holiday, murders that involve us in some way."

"I guess we're just terribly unlucky," Hope said.

River laughed. "Doesn't sound that way to me."

"How's the Christmas tree business going?" Hope asked.

"Great. Lots of people have stopped by, and some of them picked out trees. Some of them just wanted to see the place where Lauren disappeared. They don't say so, but that's the truth."

"I know. Gawkers come in all ages and sizes."

"Mom," Cori said, "River wants to know if he can come over after school tomorrow … to hang out."

Hope smiled. "Sure … after you've done your homework."

"Yeah," River said. "I have the same rule. I have to do homework right after school, unless I have to show someone a tree. Making money has to come first."

"We all understand that."

River slipped off the wall. "I have to go. There's always work to do with the trees."

"Do you need a ride?" Hope asked.

"No, thanks, my mom is picking me up. She had some errands to run."

"In that case, have a good evening."

Hope watched as River walked toward the downtown. He pulled out his phone and started tapping, the first act of almost every student in school.

"When did River take an interest in you?" Hope asked.

"Just today," Cori said. "In the cafeteria."

"Any reason why?"

"Not really. He said I was someone who didn't giggle too much."

"I suppose that's a compliment."

"It is. The gigglers are popular, but they never say anything too intelligent. It seems they laugh and giggle to put on a show."

"They might have good brains, but they're trying to be personable and popular."

"Thanks for letting River come over tomorrow. I like him. He seems like a good person."

"There are cautions I can give you, but I think you've heard them before. River seems like a nice boy who will soon be a young man. Be smart."

"I will be. He's cool. He won't try anything."

Hope wanted to give Cori a two-minute sermon on the hormonal drives of teenage girls and boys, but she refrained. There had to be a better way to help Cori navigate the shoals of teen attractions. She'd have to think about that. Maybe an example would be helpful.

"I'd appreciate it if you and River stay in the house," Hope said.

"So, Max can watch us?"

"No, he won't watch, but he will be available. That would be safe."

"All right. I guess, I should invite Lottie over, too."

"That's nice of you."

Cori chuckled. "And, she wouldn't forgive me if I didn't invite her."

"People sometimes lose a friend because a third party happened along."

"Don't I know it. I'll make it a party—me, River, Lottie, and ... Max."

Hope laughed. "When did you become so agreeable?"

"I don't know." Cori turned pensive. "There's something about River that seems just a little bit odd. I mean, he's older than me. Shouldn't he be hanging with kids his age instead of with Lottie and me?"

"Lots of friends and couples have age differences. There's no rule about that."

"I know, but it's creepy when you see some old guy with a young wife. It always seems like the wife is hoping the geezer keels over." Cori shook her head.

"It's probably not the case most of the time. And,

I hardly think a year or two is a huge age difference. Have you picked out your new laptop yet?"

"I have, and I haven't. I have three models that would work. I just have to make up my mind."

"You're the shopper. Read the reviews and make a decision."

"What if I pick the wrong one?"

"You'll have learned something. That's one benefit of picking out the wrong thing."

"I wouldn't call it a benefit, more like a mistake."

"Mistakes can be helpful. Scientists sometimes discover something useful simply because they made a mistake."

"Another teachable moment?"

"The best kind." Hope laughed.

Reaching home, Hope fielded a call from Detective Robinson.

"No word or sign of Lauren," the detective said. "We contacted her parents, who assured us that she was not the type to up and run off, at least, not by herself. I have a list of people she might contact, old school friends mostly. We're working the list now. I'll let you know if we find anything."

"Foul play seems to be becoming more likely, what with the bloody shirt and all."

"Yeah, the shirt. As I mentioned before, we found

multiple people's blood on the shirt. There is no way of knowing when the drops occurred, and there wasn't enough of it to indicate any kind of serious wound. We'll keep looking."

"I'm beginning to think that Lauren hitched a ride with a trucker or driver. What do you think about that possibility?"

"I've thought that for a while. But, if so, she's not using her phone. In fact, we can't find it. If she hitched a ride, why isn't she on her phone?"

"Good question. Young women are always on their phones, right?"

"Lauren used hers every day … a lot. We checked."

"Habits are hard to break, aren't they?"

After the conversation, Hope considered the phone. Not being as well versed in that world, she went to Cori's room. Her daughter was on the bed, reading on her laptop.

"Got a minute?" Hope asked.

"Sure. I've narrowed my search down to two. I should have an answer by morning."

"Answer?"

"I put the question to my friends, who put it to their friends. I'm letting the mob help with the decision. There's a site where you can set up a poll of sorts. People can vote for whichever computer they think is best."

"Sounds interesting. Which computer is winning?"

"It's neck and neck. Some people added comments like: None of those are any good."

"The way of the world, Cori. Hey, if you had to find a lost cell phone, could you do it?"

"Maybe, but the phone would have to be close to a tower. It would have to register with the net."

"I thought so. Lauren's phone hasn't been used since she went missing, which is one reason the police think something happened to her. These days, people are always on their phones."

"She might not have charged it, or maybe it's broken or lost."

"I know, there are lots of reasons it wouldn't be findable. Did you talk to Lottie about tomorrow?"

"Yeah, she'll be here. Don't worry, Mom, we'll outnumber River." Cori grinned.

"Good strategy."

"I'll ask my friends if they can help locate Lauren's phone. Crowd sourcing is very powerful in some ways."

"That might just work."

In the office, Max sat at the computer. He wore a

red wetsuit, as if going deep sea diving. Hope laughed.

"That can't be very comfortable," she said.

"In fact, it is not. An obvious reason no one wears a wetsuit on land. I thought I would give it a go."

"Experimentation works, for the most part."

"I have learned what not to wear."

"That's half the battle. I'll give you a heads up. Tomorrow, after school, River Soames is coming over to hang out with Cori. Lottie will be here, too. I know you're discreet, but, if you could keep an eye on them, well, that would be helpful."

"I will chaperone them religiously. However, I believe Cori has the good sense to keep things on the up and up."

"I think so, too. As she gets older, I hope she can resist whatever temptations come her way."

"You won't be here tomorrow?"

"No, I think I'll pay a visit to the Christmas tree farm."

"Have an angle of some kind?"

"Not really. It's more of a fishing expedition."

"You know, the longer the young woman is gone, the more likely it is that something bad happened to her."

"I agree, Max. Otherwise, she would surface

somewhere. She has family. She left everything behind. I'm not a big believer in amnesia. I don't think she no longer knows who she is."

"An overworked excuse, if you ask me, Mrs. Herring. While we all have things we'd like to forget, we rarely forget everything. I sometimes think that it would be a good thing if humans could be rebooted, like a computer. I've read something about computers, and how they have a basic operating system that occasionally goes haywire. In that case, the computer is restarted, and all is well."

"You make a good point, Max. Rebooting humans might be exactly what's needed. I suppose you could think of prisons as a way to reboot a person, although that's an expensive and not very successful method. Far better to update the software and start all over."

"Erase all those nasty ideas and urges that a criminal might have?"

"Interesting concept. I believe there are more than a few science fiction stories along that line. If the brain is some sort of computer, why can't we simply rewire the thing?"

"I shall give it some thought," Max said. "We might discover the download capabilities of the human mind."

Hope laughed. "I'm afraid we'd find too many people don't have the capacity to upgrade their programs."

The next day, Hope left Cori and Lottie with River and ... Max. Hope was certain Max would oversee things. Cori wouldn't need him, but he was there just in case.

The Christmas tree farm looked deserted. The magic bus was there along with the tents and lawn chairs. No one loitered on the porch. The parking lot was empty. The barn door yawned at her. She stood for a moment, looking around, then she started for the house. She had just stepped onto the porch, when Mrs. Soames stepped out.

"Can I help you?"

"I hope so. I'm Hope Herring."

"I know who you are. You're with the police. You solve all those mysteries."

"I help them from time to time. I'm really a teacher. As a matter of fact, your son is currently with my daughter at my house. There's another girl with them, so they're just fine. I was hoping to talk to you and your husband about Lauren Deinger."

"She's gone."

Hope thought the woman looked older, more worn out than when she'd seen her before. Her blond hair was dry and straight, in need of some care, and her hazel eyes were narrowed by her brows giving her a peering look, as if she were searching for something. She wore a blue T-shirt with the University of North Carolina logo on it. Hope was pretty sure the woman hadn't attended the school.

"I'm aware that she's missing, and I thought there would be deputies out here with volunteers to search the woods."

"They already did that. They didn't find anything. Like I told you, she's gone and good riddance."

"Why do you say that?" Hope cocked her head to the side.

"Because a woman like that is trouble. Don't pretend you don't know trash like her. They're always stirring up trouble, being so attractive and all."

"I know there are men and women both who can stir up jealousies, but I didn't know Lauren, so I don't know what went on when she was around."

Inside the house, a phone rang.

"I have to get that, so come on in. By the way, my name is Grace."

Hope followed Grace into the living room. She stopped as the woman headed toward what had to be the kitchen. In between was a dining room with a table loaded down with envelopes, newspapers, magazines, and several books. The room wasn't used for eating.

With Grace gone, Hope walked around the table noting the bills that were pushed messily to one corner. She couldn't tell if any of the bills were past due. It might be interesting to find out. One envelope caught her eye. It was official looking, and the return address was an IRS office. Hope stared, wondering what the IRS wanted with the Soames.

"Find something you want to read?"

17

Hope turned to find River's father staring at her.

"Just waiting for your wife to come back from taking a phone call," she explained.

Bruce Soames was tall and rangy-looking in his blue jeans and tan work boots. His green plaid shirt was sweat stained. Unruly, thin, light brown hair topped a face in need of a shave. Light blue eyes looked tired, but they held hers. Large hands bespoke the farmer's hard work.

"Maybe I can help," Bruce told her.

"Maybe, you can. I'm Hope Herring."

"I know who you are."

"I sometimes assist the police in their investigations."

"I know that, too."

"I've been asked to look into the disappearance of Lauren Deinger."

"She ran away. I think that's as simple as I can make it."

"There's a strong likelihood of that, but she doesn't seem like the type to just take off."

Bruce frowned. "She left her home up north on a moment's notice."

"That may be true, but she didn't leave alone. She came with your brother and the others in the bus."

"Doesn't mean she can't get a burr up her butt and walk off by herself."

"Not everyone has the wherewithal to abandon their lives and start over all alone."

Bruce grunted. "How do you know she was alone? She might have rode off with someone."

"That's a possibility. Did she know anyone from around here, someone she might leave with?"

"She had the Internet. A blind monkey could find someone to travel with. Someone like Lauren wouldn't have any trouble at all."

"I agree. But, would she stop using her phone? That's the problem. If she grabbed a ride with someone, why would she dump her phone?"

"Who knows? Maybe, she got another one, a

phone no one knows about. Seems to me, anyone can buy a new phone without other people knowing about it."

"All too true. You make a valid point. Can I ask you when you last saw Lauren?"

Bruce stared for a moment, as if trying to decide how much Hope already knew.

"I'm going to get a beer. You want something?"

Hope shook her head. "No thanks."

The man walked past, leaving Hope to stare at the pile of envelopes. She moved away, wondering if this were some sort of test. Did Bruce think she might become more nosey if she were alone? She waited a few minutes, and he returned, Budweiser in hand.

The man took a long draw from the beer can. "Like everyone else here, I saw Lauren the day she disappeared. Nothing special about that. I didn't see any sign that she was leaving. If she had a plan, she kept it hidden. As you know, she went off by herself and didn't come back. That's all I know about the whole thing."

"You didn't follow her?"

"Follow her? Why would I? I didn't know what she was up to. She made it pretty clear she didn't want company."

"No one went after her?"

He shook his head. "There wasn't any reason to go after her."

"Lauren was a very attractive, young woman. Conair didn't slip away after her?"

"He might have. I don't know. I don't track him. It's not like he wears some collar or something."

"Who might have had a reason to harm Lauren?" Hope asked.

Bruce's eyebrows pinched together. "Someone did something to her?"

"We don't know, but I like to explore all possibilities."

"I think everyone on that bus had a reason to dislike her. Of course, they mostly had reasons to like her, too. I'm not one to dream up stories about that."

"Did she lie?"

Bruce blinked, as if the question was totally unexpected.

"Lie? I suppose she did from time to time. Everyone lies. Did I flag her lies? Yeah, well, I might have thought there was a whopper mixed into her talk, but I never questioned her about what she said."

"No, I suppose not. Where was your wife the evening Lauren left?"

"I don't know. I was busy in the barn."

"Was there anyone in there with you?"

"Nope. I know what you're thinking. You're thinking I went after Lauren and did something to her. I didn't. My wife didn't either."

"How do you know that?'

"I know my wife. She's not one to hurt someone. That may not ring true to you, but I know it. She's a kind woman. She wouldn't hurt anyone."

"How about your brother? Would he harm someone?"

"Pete had no reason to hurt Lauren."

"I don't think you or anyone else knows for sure if Pete would harm Lauren. What I would like to know is if he might be capable of hurting her."

"I suppose he could. Pete has had his share of bar fights. That happens. It's not like he goes looking for trouble. It's just that the world is full of guys that like to smart off."

"If you know something, you should tell me. Whatever it is, it will soon come to light anyway."

"You should ask Pete about that."

"About what?"

"Rhode Island. He got in a fight in Rhode Island.

You want particulars, you ask Pete. I got to get going. I'm sure Grace will be back in a minute."

"I'm already here."

Hope turned to Grace, who didn't smile.

Pete walked out, leaving Hope alone with his wife.

"You've been listening?" Hope asked.

"I heard some."

"You said you were here in the house all alone when Lauren walked off."

Grace nodded. "Chores don't do themselves."

"Exactly. I've tried to teach my daughter that, but she believes in magic. Is your son the same way?"

"River is a good boy. He likes to dream. What boy doesn't? He does his job, even if he does complain a mite."

Hope said, "Children don't learn the value of work until they're out of the house. That's what I've discovered."

"I know I didn't," Grace agreed. "What else do you want to know?"

"Did you see anyone go after Lauren?"

Grace shook her head. "I wasn't looking, so I didn't notice. I got enough things to do without spying on anyone."

"Did Lauren ever mention anyone who might

come after her? Did she have a stalker or someone who was bothering her?"

Grace frowned. "That's a good question. If you want that answer, you'll have to ask Pete. He's the one who brought her here. If she was running away from someone, he would know. You think someone might have followed her?"

"There are people who become completely infatuated with another person. They do things they ordinarily wouldn't do. I can see where someone might chase after Lauren. She was that pretty and unattainable."

"Folks sometimes get bad notions in their heads. That could be what happened to her."

"You didn't notice any strange person around the farm?"

"We get all manner of people here all the time." Grace gave a shrug. "I wouldn't know one from the other."

"Did Lauren ever react to anyone? Did she ever seem nervous or upset when she saw someone here?"

"Not that I noticed. If you don't mind, I got things to do."

"Oh, sure, I've taken enough of your time. If you think of anything, contact me or the police."

"I'll do that. I got a question for you. Is your daughter smart?"

Hope nodded. "She's bright. Not genius material, but bright."

"That's good, cause I don't want River hanging around with people that aren't going places. I believe that a mother has to ride herd on the friends her children pick up."

"That's not a bad idea. I think most parents want to protect a child from bad influences."

"Exactly."

It wasn't until Hope was halfway home before she considered Grace's question. She had wanted to know about Cori, but what if Grace was equally curious about Lauren? Was Lauren flirting with River? Was Lauren a bad influence? Would Grace use violence to keep River and Lauren apart?

Hope didn't see how that could happen. Grace might well keep Lauren and Pete separated. The woman certainly could have followed Lauren into the trees and had some sort of confrontation that turned ugly. Grace didn't have a good alibi, but she didn't really need one. As far as anyone knew, Lauren might be sipping a Mint Julep on some Florida beach.

When Hope reached her house, she found Cori

and Max sitting side by side in the kitchen. They were both researching new laptop possibilities.

"Find what you're looking for?" Hope asked.

"Mrs. Herring, the number of available computers is absolutely staggering. They come in every possible configuration and color. You can never be sure of your choice."

"Look at it this way," Hope said. "The computer you choose will be fine. If you're going to wait for the perfect machine, you'll be waiting for the rest of your lives."

"The horse you have is better than the two you don't have," Max said.

"I still want a good laptop," Cori said.

"You'll find a good one. How was River?"

"He was an engaging boy," Max said. "He caused no problems. All went well."

"He has a crush on you, Mom," Cori said.

"What? That's hardly funny."

"Not on you exactly, on your work. He asked a ton of questions about how you solve murders."

"Why?"

"He said he's read every story about Sherlock Holmes and almost everything Agatha Christie has written. He wants to be a detective."

"Interesting. Did he have any theories about Lauren's disappearance?"

"He thinks she met someone on the highway and decided to just leave. She wasn't having much fun at the Christmas tree farm or with the others on the bus. They argued all the time."

"Did he know anything about a stalker?"

"A stalker?" Cori's eyes went wide.

"Someone who was following Lauren, or bothering her all the time. The idea just came to me recently. Lauren could have had several stalkers."

"River didn't say anything, but I can ask him. I'll send him a text."

Cori grabbed her phone and left the room.

"They got along marvelously," Max said. "The three of them seemed to hit it off."

"River was asking about murders?"

"Not an odd request, considering how many murder mysteries he's read. I was amazed myself. I, too, have read all of Doyle's works and found them fascinating. I imagine a teenage boy would be mesmerized."

Hope shrugged. "Especially an only child who lives on a farm. Reading might be the only real escape for him."

"Nothing better than a good mystery. I was

always floored by Holmes's powers of observation. He could get more information from a bit of lint than most people can glean from an encyclopedia."

"He certainly didn't make many mistakes. I'm glad the kids hit it off."

"Yes, even Lottie seemed perfectly at ease. By that, I mean she did not try to hog the limelight, if you know what I mean."

"I do. Some people have to get attention. Everyone wants attention, but some people need it more than others."

Cori reappeared. "River says that Lauren did talk about a stalker once. It was an older man who was always around. You know, like a shadow or something. She said he was spooky. He sent her a single, red rose once, for no reason at all. She told him to stop, but he didn't. He just became more secretive. She knew he was there, hanging around, watching her."

"Did River have a name for the stalker?"

"No, but he thinks she might have obtained a restraining order against him."

"The police can check that. Did she spot him down here? Did she think he followed her down here?"

"River didn't know. Oh, Lauren did tell River that

if he spotted a lime green Hyundai driving around, she wanted to know."

"Lime green? Do they even have such a color?"

"Probably a custom paint job. He said he never saw one, but he's still on the lookout."

"That's good information. All right, why don't you get started on the salads, Cori. I'm going to pass the word about the stalker to Detective Robinson. Then, we'll have dinner."

Hope took her phone to her attic office and opened her email, even as she dialed the detective.

"A stalker?" the detective asked. "I thought of that, but since she hadn't complained to anyone, I assumed the stalker had been left behind."

"She probably thought so, too. Can you check to see if she got a restraining order against someone?"

"Sure, if she did, we'll know about it."

"Oh, and a lime green Hyundai. I don't know the model, but River said Lauren asked him to keep an eye out for one."

"I'll let the patrols know. What do you think? Is this progress?"

"I don't know," Hope said. "The longer it takes to find Lauren, the colder the trail gets. I have this sneaking suspicion that she disappeared on purpose, just to cause some trouble. I expect a phone call where she asks the bus people to send her stuff."

"That would work for me."

As Hope ended the call and turned to her computer, she wondered about the stalker. Suddenly, Max appeared by the attic window.

"Someone is coming up the walk," Max told her.

18

Pete Soames took a long pull on his beer and set down the bottle.

"Thank you very much," he said. "There's nothing as refreshing as a cold beer."

Across the kitchen table, Hope smiled. "Glad you like it. Now, why did you come to see me?"

Pete ran his hand over his grizzled face. He needed a shave and a shower. In fact, his clothes needed washing. Hope supposed regular laundry didn't happen when the magic bus was in motion. She guessed he was fifty pounds overweight, with a big belly and thinning, mostly gray hair. The capillaries on his nose had burst, indicating heavy use of alcohol. He looked like someone who eased through life. He didn't worry. Something would always turn up. If not, he could live off the government for a few months. He didn't look as if he needed much—just alcohol.

"I guess I'm the last one to come to the oracle," Pete said. "You already talked to Sky and Conair, right?"

Hope nodded.

"And, I think you chatted some with my brother and Grace."

"I did."

"So, that leaves me. I'll tell you straight up that I didn't harm Lauren in any way. Yeah, I was attracted to her. I can't think of a straight man who wouldn't be. I'd guess that there are more than a few gay fellows who would like to have her for a friend. Beauty is always difficult to find."

"Did she flirt with you? Did she encourage you in any way?"

"Ah, the leading question. Did she lead me down the path like she did with Conair and my brother? Nope, I realized early on that she was more trouble than anything else. A bother I didn't need."

"So, you didn't pursue her when she walked away from the Christmas tree farm?"

"That would have been a foolish thing to do. I tried to give up being stupid many years ago. I won't say I can't do something stupid once in a while, but chasing Lauren would fall into the 'idiot' category."

"I have to say that I find you a puzzle," Hope said. "You speak well, with purpose, and yet, you clearly don't take good care of yourself."

Pete smiled. "I'm exceedingly lazy. I don't like to work. That probably strikes you as wrong. After all, there's little else on this planet but work. I used to work. I worked hard. Then, one day, I walked past a guy sitting outside his tent on the sidewalk. He was reading on his tablet computer and smoking a joint. His expensive sunglasses blocked out the bright sun. His small thermos was filled with coffee. Totally relaxed, he didn't seem to have a care in the world. Don't get me wrong. He wasn't clean. He didn't smell of cologne. He needed a shave and a haircut and clothes without holes. I stopped and asked him what he was reading. It was Faulkner, *As I Lay Dying*. That was a book I wished I had time to read. I asked him a few questions and found out that he ate three meals a day. When the weather became too cold, he would find a shelter, but that wasn't often. He collected enough welfare to pay for his joints and his alcohol. He needed very little really. Kind people often gave him money. He seemed content."

"He obviously made an impression on you."

"He told me he was the richest man on the planet. He possessed the rarest commodity on earth ... time. His time was his, it didn't belong to some corporation."

"Rich people possess time, too, don't they?"

"They do, but they also live with stress, great stress. They are always worried about their money. They live better than that guy on the sidewalk, but they fret more, too. I thought about the sidewalk guy for a while. It seemed to me that if you wanted more time, you needed to be either very rich or very poor. Obviously, achieving poverty was easier than accumulating riches."

"So, driving an old bus and living off welfare is preferable to work?" Hope questioned.

"If you hate to work. It's a tradeoff. I have time. What do most people have? Ulcers."

"What did you do after Lauren left?"

"What I always do ... nothing."

"No one was with you doing nothing?"

"No one. I don't have an alibi, but then, I don't think Lauren was harmed in any way. She got a better offer and left."

"But she left everything she owned behind."

Pete shrugged. "Which was not so much. That's a

blessing of living as we do. We acquire little. Moving on is much simpler."

Hope chatted with Pete for a few more minutes, but there was nothing more to learn from the man. After he left, she wondered how he had come to accept his chosen way of life. Was taking advantage of the welfare system really better than working? She didn't think so. Despite his love of idleness, he was still at the beck and call of the people who ran the system. If they decided to cut him off, he would have to beg or steal. He seemed smart enough to steal. She would have to ask Detective Robinson to check for outstanding arrest warrants. Hope could hardly believe Pete had never seen the inside of a jail.

"That fellow will be the ruination of this country," Max said, as he appeared in the doorway. "He was around when I was alive, just in a different body."

"You were plagued by people who refused to work?"

"I believe you can trace his kind back to Biblical times. The rule was simple in those days. If you didn't work, you didn't eat."

Hope said, "These days there's plenty of food to go around."

"That is true, but food isn't the only reward for work. I believe humans like to work, to have a purpose. Don't get me wrong. I don't believe that every person loves their work. That would be asking too much. But, most people don't like being idle. I think that the person who isn't working often picks up a hobby or two, something they enjoy doing, just to be doing it. In my day, many men liked to fish. I was never a devoted fisherman, but I knew men who were. They didn't fish for money or even food. They fished because they liked to be outside doing something ... even if they threw them back."

"Idle hands are the devil's workshop?" Hope asked.

"People with nothing to do will dream up something to occupy their time. Sometimes, what they dream up is wrong."

"I believe we're designed to move," Hope said. "We need activity. I agree with you that we all need a purpose."

"So, it would seem. Excuse me for listening, but I don't think that man has the energy to harm someone."

"Not if you believe what he says," Hope said.

"You don't?"

"I wonder if someone devoted to doing nothing

would take on the task of driving an old bus to California. Seems to me, a really lazy person would hitchhike or take a bus. Why put up with the consternations of a bus in need of constant repair?"

"So, he might have gone after that young woman?" Max questioned.

"He could have. He's smart enough to hide his true colors. He speaks well, which makes it easier to lie, I think. I'm not sure if I believe he would go to the trouble of harming the woman."

"Not even if he were jealous?"

"Of his brother? I was thinking the same thing, Max. Pete might be perfectly fine with having Lauren around … as long as she didn't pay too much attention to Bruce. Brothers do sometimes fight over the same woman, don't they?"

"Sibling rivalry is real. Men do compete, and brothers can compete harder. It's difficult to explain."

"No need. How goes the great laptop hunt?"

"Ah, yes, well, Cori and I have narrowed the search. I think she is almost ready to announce her choice."

"Terrific."

"I will leave you to your ruminations, Mrs. Herring. If you need me, I shall be in the office."

When Max disappeared, Hope asked herself why Pete had paid her a visit. Was he trying to hide something?

Hope briefed Detective Robinson over the phone. He wasn't really surprised. It seemed the people who had seen Lauren last were trying to talk to as many people as possible. He guessed they were trying to muddy the water, as if they had nothing to hide. He said he had half a mind to arrest them for drugs and let them cool in the jail for a while. Hope talked him out of that. If one of them had harmed Lauren, that person was more apt to make a mistake out of jail, not in it. The detective agreed, but he was still not releasing Conair, as he was almost guaranteed to flee.

At dinner, Cori brought up the disappearance. "You said Lauren's phone has gone dead?"

"That's right. She hasn't used it. No one has. It's off the grid."

"I asked River about that. I mean, I asked him what kind of phone she had. He said it was an ordinary iPhone, nothing special. As far as he knew, she had it with her when she left. He said she carried it around all the time just like the rest of us."

"So, it should have been pinging off cell towers, but it's not."

"If she got lost in the woods, then she might be in a dead zone. If she stayed lost, the batteries would have died by now."

"So, you're thinking she got lost. She had no connectivity, so she couldn't get help. After the phone went dead, it was only dead weight."

"She didn't have to be lost," Cori said. "She could have fallen and injured her leg or something, maybe hit her head. There are bears and coyotes and snakes and whatever in the woods. If she was unconscious..."

"You make a good point, Cori. But, hunters and hikers are in the woods all the time. No one has stumbled across her."

"Because she's at the bottom of some ravine or something. Walking around in the dark is dangerous."

"Remember that when you go hiking. Take someone with you."

"Roger that."

In bed, Hope reran her interview with Pete Soames. Something about him didn't ring true. He spoke well, but he looked like a bum. Why was that? He admitted he hadn't always been that way. He had changed for a reason. What was it? Had he ever been married? Had he ever had a serious relationship? He obviously liked women. Why did she feel he was hiding something? She promised herself she would do some digging. Had other women disappeared on his watch?

When Hope pulled up at Cori's school the next day, she found her daughter, Lottie, and River chatting while sitting on the brick wall. Cori and Lottie slipped off the wall and joined Hope.

"River doesn't need a ride?" Hope asked.

"Not today," Cori answered. "His mom is shopping. She'll pick him up."

"River asked us to come out and help him trim Christmas trees," Lottie said. "He said it's fun."

"Sounds like a way to get cheap labor," Hope said.

"Can we do it?" Cori asked. "He asked Lottie and me if we'd like to help."

"I suppose it will be all right. Figure out a good time. Maybe Saturday morning, while I'm baking."

"Sure," Lottie said. "That will work."

Hope noted how the girls grinned at each other, as if they had pulled a fast one. Hope guessed they were planning something more than just tree shaping.

"Make sure to take a look at our tree," Hope said, as they drove home.

"Aye, aye," Cori told her. "We'll make sure it's perfect."

Max greeted Hope as she entered her office. He had reverted to his jockey outfit, as if he were going to ride a horse in a race.

"Going to the Derby?" Hope asked.

"I wish I could. I just wanted something colorful."

"You are that. Has the decision been made? What laptop did you and Cori opt for?"

"She'll tell you. It's quite powerful."

Hope's phone chimed, and she answered. "Detective Robinson, what's on your mind?"

"Lauren's phone," he answered. "It's pinging."

19

"It's pinging? Are you sure?" Hope asked the detective.

"It started in Castle Park, and now it's pinging all the way to Asheville. The telephone company just called."

"She's on the move? That doesn't make any sense."

"The state police are going to try and stop her, but we don't know what car she's driving, or even if she's driving. She might be a passenger."

"How odd. Have you checked with anyone at the Christmas Tree farm? Did she contact anyone before she left?"

"I'm getting ready to do that right now. If she did

call one of them, I want to know why they didn't tell us."

"I doubt she called. Some things don't make sense, do they?" Hope asked. "I never would have thought she would leave. Any idea where she might have been staying?"

"Not a clue. However, as soon as the state police stop her, I'm going to end our investigation. I might charge her with initiating this wild goose chase."

"That might be a good idea."

"I'll keep you informed."

Hope killed the connection and tapped her phone with her finger.

"I take it the disappearance has been solved?" Max asked.

"Apparently. Lauren's phone pinged here in Castle Park, then she headed west. She's around Asheville at the moment."

"Very strange, if you ask me. She disappears for days with no trace, and then pops up for no reason. You would think she wouldn't turn on her phone until she was in the next state."

"Yes, I would expect that. It's as if she wanted us to chase her. There was no reason to use her phone. Why not just get another one?"

"Mrs. Herring, I'm certain I can't figure it out,

but I'm guessing you will. Do you think she's just playing with us? In my day, I remember a man sending a letter to a friend in Charleston. The letter contained a second letter that the friend mailed back to the man's wife. It was a ruse to convince his wife that he was in Charleston doing business."

"Postmarks are pretty good evidence, aren't they? What happened to the man?"

"His wife became suspicious, as her husband was not a prolific letter writer, so she wrote to her friend in Charleston who tried to find the husband. It didn't happen. He wasn't there."

"I suppose that led to divorce?"

"Divorce was rare in my day. The wife was not in a position to divorce her husband, so she fed him a daily dose of cyanide. Not enough to kill him outright. But, in time, it put him in his grave."

"Cyanide? How did she achieve that?"

"Apple seeds. She ground them up and put them in his food. He never noticed. It took time, but she had her revenge."

"She was caught?"

"Yes. Her husband gave a loaf of bread to a co-worker, who became sick. That event and the number of apples the wife had purchased unraveled her skullduggery. She was hanged for her handiwork."

Hope's eyes widened at that news. "Oh my, that was harsh."

"A marriage calls for a great deal of trust. To not punish someone for breaching that trust puts many people at risk. After all, people are much more apt to sin, if they know they will not pay a steep price."

"You make a good point."

Before Hope went to bed, she heard from Detective Robinson again.

"The state police missed her," he said. "She slipped into Tennessee where law enforcement tried to find her. That didn't work. Her phone stopped pinging close to Nashville."

"Stopped?"

"She either turned it off, or the battery died. We can't know which, but it's no longer making contact with cell towers."

"That's very curious," Hope said. "She's like the pied piper. She leads us on a merry chase and then disappears. I don't get it."

"I think it might have been a mistake, like a butt call. She managed to turn on her phone without knowing it. Then, when she discovered it was on, she turned it off."

"Did you check on the others at the farm?"

"I did, but they claim Lauren made no calls to them."

"Exactly. But, they're all there?"

"Yes, why?"

"What if Lauren didn't leave? What if she was kidnapped? She's been held until it was safe to move her. Somehow, she started her phone, perhaps in the hope someone would notice and rescue her. When her abductors discovered the phone, they turned it off."

"I hadn't thought of that. Why would they take her out of state?"

"She's very pretty, gorgeous. Human trafficking? Would someone pay to have her?"

"She's certainly attractive enough. I don't know of any trafficking rings around here, but that doesn't mean they don't exist."

"I ... I don't really think it's that. I'm just spit balling, tossing out weird explanations for a weird event. Occam's razor."

"What?" the detective asked.

"Occam developed a famous rule on how to solve problems. He said that the simplest solution was usually the best. In this case, Lauren wasn't taken. For whatever reason, she decided to disappear for a few days, before she left for good. Her phone came alive, and she left a trail. It's probably that simple."

"You're probably right. I'll have to remember Occam when my people start to speculate on what might have happened. You should hear some of the stuff they dream up. They can turn simple teenage graffiti into an international attack."

"Humans like convoluted explanations. Simplicity is too easy."

Hope went to bed with her mind filled with Lauren's flight. While she believed that less was more when it came to mysteries, she couldn't find a good reason for Lauren to leave town the way she did. Why would she leave everything behind? Why would she turn on her phone? Why would she turn it off? Hope guessed that Lauren had found a friend, someone with a car. That made sense. Lauren made friends easily. That friend would certainly offer to take Lauren along for a cross-country ride.

But why would Lauren leave the others?

Hope wished Lauren had made a call from her phone. All it did was ping towers. No conversations or surfing.

A mistake?

Hope couldn't come up with anything more simple than that. But what if Lauren had been kidnapped? Or what if someone killed her and took her phone, and they made the mistake of turning it on?

Detective Robinson did not close the investigation since no one had actually seen Lauren, but he did move his assets to other cases. He saw no reason to find a woman who didn't want to be found. Since no corpse had appeared, and she had left Castle Park, he considered the case all but solved.

Hope had to agree, although Lauren didn't surface in Nashville. Her phone was cold again. The local police had a photo, but no one had spotted her. Of course, Nashville was a big city with many, many people. Finding Lauren was near impossible. Hope tried to push the pretty woman from her mind. That little mystery had been solved. Or had it?

On Saturday, Lottie's mom drove the girls to the Christmas tree farm where they were turned over to River. Adele waited until the girls and River had climbed onto an ATV and disappeared into the trees, before she turned around and returned home. Hope was on her hands and knees weeding a flower bed, when Adele arrived.

"Mission accomplished," Adele said.

"I made a mistake," Hope said.

"What mistake? They're not safe?"

"No, no, I should have kept Cori home, so she could help with the weeding. My back is killing me."

"Then, it's time to take a break. Ibuprofen and wine will do away with the pain."

"You have no idea how tempting that sounds, but, the beds won't weed themselves."

"I hear you. All right, we'll do it this way. You get to work one more hour. Then, you're coming to my house for the cure. Don't argue. I'll be expecting you."

"I might not be finished in an hour."

"This is North Carolina, you'll never be rid of weeds. We have weeds for all seasons, including winter. One hour, then I'll ding your phone."

Hope gave her friend a smile. "You win. I'll be there."

Adele left, and Hope returned to her weeds, but she did keep track of the time. In fact, she checked her phone every ten minutes. Why did time not fly when she was weeding? The day dragged by. When her hour of torture ended, she was happier than she had been in days. She ran to the shower and was fit for polite company in record time. Those minutes flew by.

Adele handed Hope a glass of Chardonnay. "I

should have told you to come as you were. Now, you smell better than me."

"I don't smell as good as this wine. I can tell you that."

Adele led Hope to the patio where the glass-topped table was loaded with cheese and crackers.

"You might have showered," Adele said, "but, I'm willing to bet you didn't eat."

"I'm starving," Hope said and picked up a small plate. "Thank you so much."

"It's nothing. Have you heard from the girls?"

"Not a chance. I don't expect anything until we pick them up."

"Or, if there's a problem. I have to confess I've been naughty. I've been tracking them."

"Tracking them?"

"There's an app that allows you to find a device, no matter where it is, provided it's connected to the net somehow. Since the trees are on the net, so are the phones. Here, look."

Adele showed her phone, and Hope noticed the little, blue dot that identified Lottie's phone.

"I tell myself it's not spying," Adele said. "Lottie will turn off her phone if she doesn't want me to know where she is. That's a problem. We've had a talk, but she doesn't obey well all the time."

"You'll have to wean yourself off the app. Once they start driving, they'll never want you to know where they've been."

"Oh gosh, she's going to be like me. I never told my mother where I was going. Well, I did, but I lied. I told myself she didn't need to know where I went. I was a snot when I was in high school."

Hope said, "You weren't the only one. Sometimes, I think they put some kind of drug in the water, something that turned us into stupid liars."

"I used to think I fooled my parents, but I didn't," Adele admitted. "They knew. They were simply too kind or too tired to call me on every fib."

Hope held up her glass. "To having decent parents, who didn't lock us in our rooms until we turned twenty-five."

Adele clicked her glass with Hope's, and they sipped.

"Can you tell if the girls are close to the trees we picked out?" Hope asked.

"I can try." Adele pulled out her phone and started tapping. "I don't know how to use both apps at once, but I think I can find the trees."

Hope looked over the still-green lawn. In a few months, the grass would go dormant and turn tan. The leaves would fall, and the view would turn stark. Not as stark as it had been in Ohio. Still, it would be winter, and winter, with its short days, was always a trial.

"Shoot," Adele said. "I have the wrong code."

"That's right, the first tag failed, didn't it?"

"Wait, I have the new code. River sent me a text message with it." Adele thumbed through her messages quickly. "I should organize these things. No, I should delete a bunch of messages. I guess I'm a packrat. I don't want to lose something I might need."

"The messages are never lost. That's the beauty and curse of the Internet. It has a memory that won't quit."

"Here it is. No, wait, that was the second one."

"Second one?" Hope asked.

"You remember. The whatever you call it didn't work, so River put a second one on the tree. That one didn't work either."

"He put a third tag on your tree?"

"Yes, and here it is." Adele smiled. "A few taps and, yep, there's my tree. All safe and ready."

Hope thought a second. "Try the second code."

"What? Why? River said that one didn't work."

"Please, just try it."

"You want to make sure it doesn't work? It's not like River charged me for it."

"Adele, please just do it."

Adele rolled her eyes and used the second code. "That's funny. It's working now."

"What does it show?"

"A tree at the opposite end of the farm. He must have fixed it and used it for another customer."

With a look of purpose on her face, Hope stood. "Don't finish your wine. We're leaving."

"What?"

"You're driving. Come on."

20

"All right," Adele said, "why am I driving hellbent for the Christmas tree farm?"

"Our daughters are there."

"I know that, but, they're with River. I think they're in good hands."

"I'm not so sure."

"Please explain."

"It's all about the electronic tag that River said didn't work."

"It didn't work."

"We don't know that for sure." Hope stared through the windshield at the road.

"Of course, we do. It failed, remember?"

"That was the first tag. You couldn't connect to it."

"Right. Then, the second tag failed."

"We don't know that."

Adele frowned. "Why don't we know that? River told me it didn't work."

"Exactly. But it does work. We just proved that."

"So? He fixed it. That's not hard to believe."

"What if it never failed?" Hope asked.

"But it did."

"River said it did," Hope corrected her.

"Why would he lie?" Adele took a turn onto another road.

"Precisely, why would he lie?"

"You're not going to tell me, are you?"

"Not yet. I don't want to say something that isn't true."

"I hope you know what you're doing."

Hope took a deep breath. "No one hopes more than I do."

The magic bus hadn't moved. Pete and Sky sat next to it, sipping beer and looking at nothing in particular. Hope ignored them. She marched to the door of the farmhouse and knocked. Grace came to the door.

"Can I help you?" the woman asked.

"Have River and our daughters come back from trimming the trees?"

"Not yet, why?"

"Do you know where they are?"

"In the trees."

"Where's your husband?"

"In the trees."

"Can you call him?"

"Why?"

"Because, I want to get my daughter off the farm before I call the police."

Grace stared, her face hard. "What kind of stunt are you trying to pull?"

"I hope I'm terribly wrong, but I don't think so. Please, call your husband."

"Wait here."

Hope walked to the edge of the porch with Adele in tow.

"You have to start talking soon." Adele's face was lined with worry. "What are we doing out here?"

"If I'm right, we're going to find Lauren Deinger."

"I thought she left, and headed west."

"A lot of people think she did." Hope stared out at the trees growing in rows.

"I heard that her phone pinged from here to Denver."

"Nashville, and you're right, it did."

"Then, she must be in Nashville."

"Her phone is in Nashville," Hope pointed out. "I don't think she is."

"I don't think she just let someone take her phone," Adele said.

"She didn't. Someone wanted us to think she went to Nashville. That was the big mistake, the phone, and our misinterpretation of what it meant."

"First, you say the tag that failed really didn't fail. Now, you're saying Lauren didn't go to Nashville. What does it mean?"

Grace reappeared on the porch. "He's on his way, and he's not happy about it."

"Neither am I." Hope managed to hold Adele at bay as they waited for Bruce Soames to arrive. It wasn't long. True to Grace's words, Bruce was anything but happy. He climbed off his ATV and clomped to the porch.

"What the heck are you thinking?" he asked. "I got work to do."

Hope turned to Adele. "Show him the tag."

"Which one?"

"The one that doesn't mark your tree."

Adele pulled out her phone, punched in a code, and showed the screen to Bruce Soames.

"Where is that tag located?" Hope demanded.

Bruce frowned. "On the other side of the creek."

"Still part of your farm?"

"Yeah, but it's not being used. More like a trash heap, if you know what I mean."

"Can you take us there?"

"Why?" Bruce scowled at Hope. "Because there's a tag that got thrown away and still works?"

"I don't think it was thrown away, but we have to go there."

"We might be too late," Bruce told them. "I told River to burn the heap. He and your daughters were headed that way."

"Let's go." Hope headed for the ATV. "We may not have much time."

Bruce didn't move.

"If I have to drive myself, I will," Hope said.

Bruce stomped over to the ATV, even as Adele scrambled into the back.

"Please call the sheriff and Detective Robinson," Hope told Grace. "Tell them to come here. Tell them I know what's going on."

Bruce drove fast, but not recklessly. Hope held on, as did Adele.

"You better know what you're doing." Bruce yelled over the sound of the engine.

"I think I do. Tell me, did the people looking for Lauren search the trash heap?" Hope spoke loudly.

"What for? Her shirt was on the opposite side of the farm."

"Exactly."

In a few minutes, they came to a shallow creek. Bruce didn't hesitate, and splashed across.

"Just a bit longer," he said.

There was a rough trail that led to the top of a hill. The ATV bounced all over, but Hope and Adele managed to hang on. At the top of the hill, Bruce stopped.

The glade ahead of them was half full of limbs, logs, trunks, leaves, needles, roofing shingles, and all the flotsam and jetsam that came with a farm operation. Hope looked and knew it would make a dandy bonfire.

Between Hope and the pile was another ATV, and next to it stood Lottie and Cori. They watched as River doused part of the pile with gasoline. In a few seconds, he was going to light a fire.

"Don't let him set it on fire," Hope shouted.

"Why the heck not?" Bruce questioned.

"Because, if I'm right, Lauren's body is in that pile."

"You're insane."

"Go, Go! Before he can do it."

The ATV charged down the hill, and as it skidded to a stop, Hope jumped off.

"Mom?" Cori looked shocked to see her mother running toward her.

"Mom?" Lottie echoed, with the same look on her face.

Hope didn't stop to explain, but ran as fast as she could to River. The boy was holding a book of matches near a bundle of papers.

"Put it down," Hope yelled at the teen.

River looked over. "I have to burn it."

"It won't do any good." Hope stepped closer.

"What are you talking about?" River demanded.

"I'm talking about Lauren."

His eyes widened in fear.

Hope said to him, "You think that burning the pile will turn her into ashes. That won't happen, River. There will be remains, and the coroner will identify them. They'll know this is where you hid the body."

"I don't..."

"Yes, you do. I believe you didn't mean to kill her. You saw her head into the trees, and you thought it was a good chance to talk to her, to tell her how you felt. I understand. You're a young teen wanting a beautiful woman that wasn't that much older than you. You thought she would want you in the same way. She didn't. She wasn't nice. She made you angry, so angry you did something."

River's face hardened. "I have to burn it."

The girls approached, as did Bruce and Adele.

"No, you don't," Hope told him. "That will only make things worse. You see, River, I don't think you intended to kill her. It just happened. You thought hiding the body would be the best thing to do. After all, she was someone who didn't have a home or maybe not even a family. People would think she ran off. That was why you took her bloody shirt and planted it by the highway, as far from here as possible."

River took a step toward the pile, ripped out a match, and lit it.

"Stop," Bruce said. "Put the match down."

"Dad…"

"You heard me. If she's in there … put it down."

River looked from face to face. For a few seconds, Hope thought he would obey. He faked a move to drop the papers, but used the match to set them on fire, then made a leap and ran toward the trash pile.

Cori was the one who tripped him. He might have thought the girls wouldn't react in time. He was wrong. He fell, and the burning papers flew apart.

Before River could stand, Bruce was towering over his son. Hope, Adele, Cori, and Lottie stomped out the fire. When Hope stopped and looked, River was sobbing on his father's shoulder.

"How did you know?" Cori asked breathlessly.

"I didn't, not until Lauren's phone made its cross-country trip. That was River's ploy to add complexity to the crime."

"I don't get it. How did he do it?"

"I think he simply dropped it onto some semi heading west. The phone kept pinging until the battery died. But there were no calls out, no connections, no texts, no searches, nothing. Would someone like Lauren travel for hours without using her phone?"

"But, how did you know about the trash pile?"

"When River moved the body here, he managed to drop the tag he was going to put on Lottie's tree. There was no way to find it in the dark. So, he activated a new tag and put that on the tree. There was no reason for anyone to look for the lost tag, and it would disappear in the flames when he set the pile on fire. And, he was right. Lottie and her mom didn't try to contact that lost tag. No one did. His mistake? Giving the code to Adele before he actually put the tag on the tree."

Hope heard the sirens in the distance. Soon, the site would be overrun with law enforcement.

"He should have fessed up," Cori said with anger in her voice.

"He panicked."

"Well, sometimes, you have to own up for what you've done."

Hope hugged her daughter. "It's a valuable lesson."

21

"Bravo, Mrs. Herring." Max beamed at her. "You've outdone yourself yet again."

"Hardly, and I'm sorry it came out the way it did."

Hope sat at the kitchen table with Max. He was wearing a tuxedo, which he said was in honor of her triumph.

"Did you always suspect him?" Max patted Bijou who was curled up on his lap.

"A little. He didn't have an alibi, but then, he didn't need one since he was a teenager. No one really thought him capable. But he was. He was more than strong enough. Still, it was an awful stretch to consider him a viable suspect."

"I am reminded of an event back in my day. A family not too far from here perished in a fire. It was winter, and they had several fireplaces. Everyone assumed an ember had escaped the fire box and landed on something flammable. Houses in my time were little more than tinder boxes. They turned to ashes in minutes. Of course, our fire brigade was none too lively, especially on a cold night. A family of five. They all died, except for the youngest, a boy of five. He managed to crawl out a window. He broke his leg in the fall. Everyone felt sorry for him because he had lost everything, family and home. It wasn't until decades later, after he had been unsuccessful at everything he had tried to do that he drank himself to death."

Max paused and looked out the window. He turned back, his face saddened.

"I sat with him that last night. I found him on a lawn, passed out. I roused him and brought him here, to this kitchen. I could have turned him over to the police, but he'd had more than a fair number of run-ins with them. They would just lock him in a cell until he passed through the delirious part of his withdrawal. Someone plagued with deliriums is no one to envy. Anyway, it was here, as he became slightly more sober that he told me how he was playing with matches when the family house caught fire. The others were all asleep. He tried to put out the fire, but he was only five. He only made it worse. In the end, he ran through the smoke to his parents. It was too late. He went out the window."

"What an awful story."

"Made worse by the fact that he didn't tell anyone. He lived with a guilt that disappeared only when he drank. He had killed his parents and siblings. He wanted to die."

"What did you do?"

"Help him along? No, no, although I thought about it. To me, it would have been a mercy. I did the next best thing. I set two bottles of corn whiskey in front of him and went to bed. He passed away sometime during the night."

"A mercy."

"He had confessed. He could move on. People are like that. If they can't resolve their guilt, they torture themselves."

"Some do. There are some that feel little if any guilt. They don't suffer. They create suffering for others."

Cori entered and placed a printed page on the table in front of Hope. "There it is, the laptop I'd like to have."

"If I could," Max said, "I would buy it for you."

"I know, Max. Ghosts don't have money because

they don't need any." Cori grinned at the ghost. "How convenient."

Max laughed.

With a smile, Hope looked from Cori to Max, and she knew that she was blessed.

And then she wished something that could never come true ... she wished neither of them would ever leave her.

THANK YOU FOR READING!

Books by J.A. Whiting can be found here:
amazon.com/author/jawhiting

To hear about new books and book sales, please sign up for our mailing list at:
jawhiting.com

Your email will never be sold, shared, or spammed.

If you enjoyed the book, please consider leaving a review. A few words are all that's needed. It would be very much appreciated.

BOOKS BY J.A. WHITING & NELL MCCARTHY

HOPE HERRING PARANORMAL COZY MYSTERIES

TIPPERARY CARRIAGE COMPANY COZY MYSTERIES

BOOKS BY J. A. WHITING

SWEET COVE PARANORMAL COZY MYSTERIES

LIN COFFIN PARANORMAL COZY MYSTERIES

CLAIRE ROLLINS PARANORMAL COZY MYSTERIES

MURDER POSSE PARANORMAL COZY MYSTERIES

PAXTON PARK PARANORMAL COZY MYSTERIES

ELLA DANIELS WITCH COZY MYSTERIES

SEEING COLORS PARANORMAL COZY MYSTERIES

OLIVIA MILLER MYSTERIES (not cozy)

SWEET ROMANCES by JENA WINTER

COZY BOX SETS

BOOKS BY J.A. WHITING & ARIEL SLICK

GOOD HARBOR WITCHES PARANORMAL COZY MYSTERIES

BOOKS BY J.A. WHITING & AMANDA DIAMOND

PEACHTREE POINT COZY MYSTERIES

DIGGING UP SECRETS PARANORMAL COZY MYSTERIES

BOOKS BY J.A. WHITING & MAY STENMARK

MAGICAL SLEUTH PARANORMAL WOMEN'S FICTION COZY MYSTERIES

HALF MOON PARANORMAL MYSTERIES

VISIT US

jawhiting.com

bookbub.com/authors/j-a-whiting

amazon.com/author/jawhiting

facebook.com/jawhitingauthor

bingebooks.com/author/ja-whiting

J A WHITING
Books and More

Printed in Great Britain
by Amazon